JOY *of* LIVING

JOY *of* LIVING

DR RICHA SAXENA (MD)

PARTRIDGE
A Penguin Random House Company

Cover photo Courtesy: S. Balasubramanyam

To order additional copies of this book, contact
Partridge India
000 800 10062 62
orders.india@partridgepublishing.com

www.partridgepublishing.com/india

DEDICATION

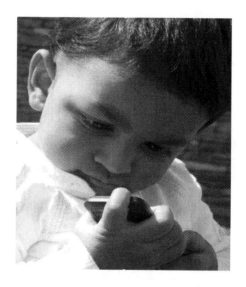

To my 5-year-old nephew Akshar Saxena,
whose continuous kiddish persuasions and cajoling helped
me in completing this project despite of a hectic schedule.

Contents

Author's Note

The characters, events and firms depicted in this story are a complete work of fiction. Resemblance to any person living or dead is purely coincidental.

Picture Courtesy: Debjeet Kundu

PROLOGUE

Carol was busy practicing for her next singing assignment. Just as she glanced through the window, she realized that there were no stars in the sky. The sun was shining brightly and a fierce wind was blowing. What caught her attention was a loud chirping of birds, all of them perched on a rope tied over the water of a nearby pond. Carol could not stop herself from observing their actions. They were all trying to fly towards the sky. In the process, some fumbled, fell back over the rope. Nonetheless, they all continued to try even after falling back several times. She continuously kept observing their action and felt that this message was meant for her. She smiled at herself and continued practicing her music lessons.

"We do not see things as they are
We see them as we are"

—*The Talmud*

CHAPTER 1

Distinct Individuals

Carol rushed up the stairs. She did not want to be late. In fact she had never been this late. Today, there had been an accident on the highway and so the traffic was unusually slow. She knew this was no excuse she could give, especially for her first meeting at her new job today at "Planners and Designers", an architecture firm. She had been lucky enough to get a job within a month of completing her graduation and internship in architecture. Most of her bachmates were still struggling for a job, appearing for the job interviews and making efforts for improving their portfolios. She had been the lucky one . . . . to get a job at a big firm, which she had now been doing since past one month.

Carol had been born with a silver platter . . . . her father, David Wilde, was a well-known figure amongst the circle of architects. Carol still had vivid memories of watching her father spend several hours while designing a building on a sheet of paper. Since her childhood she too had aspired to be an architect so that she could think, design, and create just like she had always seen her father doing. These were only few of the memories about her father, which she deeply cherished. She did not even want to think about most other memories about her father, which she had since her young age. Even though her father was a successful architect and owner of a large architecture firm, titled D&W firm, he had hardly contributed anything for managing the household. Her mother, Judy was trained in classical music and would earn some money by teaching music to a group of young people. Carol could not remember if she ever looked towards her father for any kind of emotional support. As far as she could remember from the period of her childhood, things had never been fine between her parents. It was just that they had still not applied for divorce and were living together under one roof. However, Carol wished they had separated. Every other day there were episodes of her father getting violent after getting drunk. Many a times she had to call police so that her father would not harm her mother or herself. Carol had often persuaded her mother to apply for divorce. However, she would always refuse and say that she would never leave David as long as she was alive. Since an early age, Carol had pledged that she would take her father's place in the family and provide financial and emotional support to her mother. Meanwhile, Carol herself had always been close to her mother. So her relationship with her father had also become quite strained. She never wanted to pretend a false relationship with her father, but she had really stopped thinking about him.

Despite of all this she had always aspired to be an architect. "Job of an architect comprises of long working hours and crappy salary", many people had told her. However, one thing was clear in her mind, she shall never use her father's name to achieve her dreams. She would do that all by herself . . . . Create a place for herself all by her own. Today, at last after 5 gruelling years at the architecture school and 1 year of unpaid internship, she was finally there. Well, she realized that she was almost there, just 10 minutes late.

She was well aware of how she had procured this job at her own credit. She remembered doing an unpaid internship at a college just to build-up her contacts. She did not know how to react when her friends would make fun of her saying, "why do you need to build your contacts and work for anyone, when you can very well use your dad's contacts."

"I want to be known by own merits and not by that of my dad," she would tell them. At times, however, it was difficult for her to deal with such negative comments, but she was determined to continue working for free with a hope that one day she might accomplish what she had always aspired for, on her own.

While she was fumbling up the stairs to reach the presentation room, she glanced up towards the clock displayed on the wall to check the time. As she hurried up the stairs, she missed a step and fell down. All the files and papers she had been carrying scattered all over the floor. As she scanned the area, a few beads of perspiration appeared on her forehead. She was already late and now all this. Suddenly she saw a young man stop by. She was pleasantly surprised as the stranger bent down to help her pick up the scattered files and papers and clear up the mess and she continued to stare at him in mute silence. "Here are your files", he handed over the pile to her.

"I am getting late for an urgent meeting, see you soon", said the stranger as he tried to hurriedly hand over the files to Carol.

She instinctively took the pile from him and muttered, "thank you", which was barely audible. She had never met the stranger before, but he appeared to know her. Forcing herself not to think about the stranger at that time, she checked the watch again and swiftly moved towards the presentation room. She knocked and slowly opened the door. Her heart skipped a beat as she entered inside the room. Presentations had already started; she silently walked towards the group of people standing at the side of the stage. As she mutely looked up at the presenter, her thoughts started wandering. She started thinking about the young stranger who had helped her on the staircase. She tried to mentally visualise him. He had a dark complexion with dark coloured eye brows.

Carol was lost in her thoughts when she felt somebody tapping her shoulder. She turned back, it was the assistant manager, John, saying, "Carol, your presentation is next, be ready." Abruptly aroused from her trail of thoughts, she mumbled, "hmmm . . . yes." Suddenly she felt guilty about what she had been thinking about. She silently scolded herself for thinking about anything else except her presentation. Once again she reminded herself of her aim in life, to become a very successful architect. She had to become successful for her mother and herself.

"Ladies and gentlemen, the next presentation would be by Miss Carol Wilde". As soon as Carol heard this, she quickly marched up to the podium with the laptop in her hands. This was the first design meeting she had been attending in this office. She had been working on the construction drawings since last month for this project. In this job, Carol was involved in the artistic side of the building construction process: sketching freehand designs, making initial computer generated images of her designed sketches, and putting together presentations for clients. Sketching and designing had always been her passion. This was one of the things about being an architect, which she loved the most. Even at the architecture school, she would spend hours together at the design studio, spending hours at a stretch making designs while listening to the music.

Music had been Carol's another passion. In fact, the art of music had come to her naturally from her mother, Judy.

Carol was happy that her presentation went off well. She realized that the audience had actually liked the designs she had made. Following the end of presentation meeting, she hoped to meet the construction manager, Rex Harrison, who was supposed to join from that day. Rex required a senior designer who could handle construction drawings, because he himself would be too busy with frequent trips to construction sites, observation of construction details, client meetings, etc. Rex was a licenced architect and Carol would be working under him as a senior designer. After her presentation, Carol felt sad that Rex was not there at the time of presentation. "What kind of irresponsible person is Rex? He is late for his first meeting", Carol thought. Previously, she had been looking forward towards working with Rex. "He is very hardworking and intelligent," John, who had previously worked with Rex, had told her. Now she really doubted what he had told her.

During the lunch time, John told her that Rex had come and he wanted to meet her.

Carol quickly finished her lunch and walked towards Rex's cabin.

"May I come in?" asked Carol politely.

It was a nod and not even a proper yes, as Carol walked in. She could not see anyone. It was a head engrossed deep in some paper work. "How will I ever work with a person who does not even have the time to look at me", pondered Carol.

"You would like something, some tea or coffee?" Rex asked her.

"No, thanks, I just had my lunch", quickly replied Carol.

Carol started thinking, "Just tea, he could have asked some genuine questions, like which college you graduated from? What are your future plans in this line, etc . . . . etc. He has not even asked for my portfolio. He does not want to know the kind of designs I am capable of making. He did not bother to come for the meeting either. Is he really serious about working?"

"So you are David Wilde's daughter", Rex casually asked, forcing Carol to come out of her thoughts.

Carol was suddenly taken up by surprise. "He knows my father. Probably he thinks that I have come through him."

"Yes, I am", replied Carol sternly. "However, I have come here through my own merit and not through my father's contacts."

"Oh, yes, I have heard a lot about your self-respect, integrity and dignity", replied Rex sounding bored.

"What's wrong with that", asked Carol defending herself.

"I never said that there is something wrong with that", Rex quickly replied.

"How do you know my father?", asked Carol trying to slightly change the topic.

"I used to work with him, many years back, my first job was with him," Rex answered.

Carol was not sure if Rex was speaking the truth. She wanted to see his facial expressions. She bent sideways to get a glimpse of him. However, she could not really see him; there was a pile of paper on the table which obscured her view. Carol realized that he was deeply engrossed in something. Their first joint project, she presumed. After a while of looking at the papers and other things scattered on the table, she started staring at the wall behind him.

"His table is so highly disorganized, I am sure his work is equally disorganized. How would we ever get along together at work", thought Carol. Her thoughts drifted towards the designs she had made and which she had thought she would discuss with Rex. She thought about the hard work she had put in the whole night to work on those designs. Suddenly Rex stood up as if he had read her thoughts. He was talking to someone on his mobile phone. Now, Carol could see him. As soon as Carol saw Rex, she thought to herself, "I have seen him somewhere; I think it is the same dark-coloured complexion and dark coloured hair I had seen sometime earlier during the day." Then it struck her suddenly like a bolt of thunder. Rex was the same stranger who had helped her in the morning when she had dropped all her files and papers while climbing up the stairs. He had been so helpful to her, even though they were complete strangers to each other at that time. "So probably Rex had already known about me and he had been very much in the office for the presentation meeting", mused Carol. She remembered that he had to suddenly leave because of some urgent meeting. Perhaps, Rex was not as bad as she had been portraying him to be. Carol rebuked herself for thinking so unpleasantly about Rex.

"So the meeting is fixed for tomorrow", Carol was suddenly drawn towards the present as she heard Rex saying this to the person he was speaking to over the phone.

Just as Carol had begun to wonder if the fixed meeting had been related to her, she heard Rex telling her, "Miss . . . ." suddenly searching for words to speak.

Carol, promptly replied, "Carol, Carol Wilde".

At the same time in her mind she loudly retorted, "Great, he does not even remember my name now."

"Yes, Miss Carol Wilde", said Rex trying to sound as formal as possible. "So see you tomorrow at Oak Street, sharp 9 am. That is the project site."

"Oh sure, I shall be there!", answered Carol with a weak smile.

"O God, this man had been all this while discussing about our project only and I thought that he had been ignoring me. But he should have at least said so," thought Carol.

Carol feeling a little embarrassed about the way she had been thinking about Rex, turned to say good bye.

"Bye, see you tomorrow", Carol turned just to see Rex standing near the window with his back turned towards her.

Carol was most disgusted to observe that there had been no response on the part of Rex.

As Rex observed Carol swiftly moving out, through the window of his cabin, a striking resemblance to Jane struck him. He could not help notice Carol's sharp features, soft eyes and lovely smile. Years back, he had met Jane while he was doing graduation in architecture. It had been love at the first site for both of them. What had initially started as a passionate love story had sadly ended amidst tears, and much pain.

He sadly smiled at himself just to hide the pain which had now started gnawing him from inside. He gently criticized himself for thinking about all this.

Carol was just another employee of the firm who would be working under him. Why should he think of his past even if this girl had a strikingly similar appearance to Jane. "We are just going to be work mates," Rex convinced himself. "Let's see what tomorrow holds," thought Rex as he closed his backpack.

"First tell yourself what you want to be;
And then do what you need to do"

—*Epictetus (55-c.135), Greece*

CHAPTER 2

A New Beginning

B right sunshine welcomed the day. Even though the sun was shining bright, it was particularly cold for this part of the year. Cool breeze was blowing which was making her silky black hair fly in the air. She briskly walked down the road, which led towards the construction site on the Oak Street. She was really excited about this. Here would be her first practical assignment. Every nerve and muscle in her body was yearning to do its best to bring out the best possible design for the building at the proposed site. She had been well prepared for hard work in extreme conditions during her graduation and final exams. In fact, she was striving to do work, some good quality work.

Whether she was striving to work with Rex, well, she was still not too sure about that.

Though she was half-jittery with excitement, somewhere at back of her mind there hit a strong doubt about whether she would be able to get along well with Rex. Normally, she never really had problems dealing with people. In fact she felt that most people with whom she interacted liked her. Well, however, Rex was different . . . . and difficult mainly because she felt that he did not believe in interacting with others. Still, she was not really sure of him.

"Think of the devil and devil is there", she thought with a smile as she heard Rex's voice and saw his shadow, looming at the construction site. Though she was still far from the site to be able to see Rex clearly, she recognized him through his loud voice. He did not appear to be shouting. He was probably just discussing his plans with one of the civil engineers at the site.

As Carol approached Rex, she was able to obtain a clearer view. She could not help, but notice Rex in the broad sunshine of the day. Today she realized that he was tall, well-built and muscular. As she approached even closer, she observed his well-formed facial bone structure and chiselled jawline. His dark thick hair was also swaying with the wind. "Strangely, today his eyes also appear to be exuding some kind of understated kindness", Carol noticed. She was surprised to note that she actually found him handsome. She was genuinely surprised because this was the last thing she had expected after having the meeting with him yesterday, where he was slouching on the chair and there had been hardly any eye contact between the two. As Carol was continuously looking at Rex, he caught her eye and waved back. She was again surprised because this was hardly what she had expected from him.

"He is good-looking and is trying to be friendly as well," Carol mused.

She was genuinely surprised. Rex then introduced her to the civil engineer, Jack and the planning assistant, Amy. All of them soon sat down on the table in the lawn area to discuss their plans. Today was the day full of surprises for Carol. However, it was not all that bad because the day passed in a jiffy. The whole day, Carol was busy designing, planning, developing and discussing her plans with Jack and Amy. When she looked at her watch, it was already 4 pm, time for the office to finish. She waved goodbye to Jack and Amy. Rex had already told her that he would be leaving with her so that she could drop him to the hostel. Rex's parents Richard and Alice Harrison lived in Pennsylvania. Rex had moved to New York due to his work commitments, so he lived in a bachelor's accommodation in the boys hostel.

Carol stayed with her parents in a house on the Ivy Street.

There was hardly any conversation between Rex and Carol as Rex drove back. Though Carol was the owner of the vehicle, she had shown extra courtesy to Rex by asking him if he would drive. After all, she felt that he was elder to her and her senior at work. She decided to give him some extra respect. Anyway, he had not been so arrogant as he had been yesterday. In fact he had fully supported Carol in her designs and plans today.

While accepting the car keys, Rex said. "I am not really confident because I have never driven this particular model of the car."

Carol replied, "I don't mind unless you break my car."

Rex quietly assured her that such a situation would never arise. As they headed back home there was hardly any conversation between Carol and Rex. It was not that Carol wanted to avoid Rex. Rather she was happy that the day had passed without any argument between Rex and herself. Until today morning, she had been completely sure that it might be very difficult to work with Rex. However, today he had been completely different from what he had been yesterday. Though she had been quiet during most part of the journey, she could not help laughing out really hard when he fumbled while changing the gears. He felt awkward when she suddenly started laughing, but soon he joined Carol in her laughs.

While driving on the way, Carol asked Rex, "How do you manage all alone? I believe your family does not stay here with you. Isn't it difficult to stay alone?"

"Sure it is difficult, sometimes it gets very lonely and I have to do everything on my own, even if I am not well or you just don't feel like doing it. Why do you ask?" Rex questioned Carol.

Carol was suddenly caught off-guard. "Oh, I was just concerned for you. I have never stayed alone in my life till now, so I was just asking. I am sorry for asking you like that," said Carol.

"You don't have to be sorry, Carol. I am just not used to anybody showing concern to me so I reacted abruptly", quietly replied Rex.

"Okay cut it, friends all right?" Carol said holding her right hand out. She did not want to get into an argument with Rex towards the end of the day.

"Yes, definitely", said Rex, grasping her hand warmly with his right hand.

"Wow, what beautiful flowers", Carol said suddenly upon noticing a small flower shop on the side of the road.

"Lets seal our friendship with some flowers", said Carol, stopping her car in front of a flower shop."

"Why suddenly flowers?" Rex asked genuinely surprised.

"Because I love them", said Carol spontaneously. "And I think that they would brighten up your gloomy room. Don't you think so?"

"Actually I never thought that one day I would be keeping flowers in my room. Besides, nobody has ever presented me flowers," replied Rex with his face reddened with embarrassment.

"Don't get so embarrassed Rex," Carol said sweetly. "It won't be so bad. I am sure you will be happy when you look at them."

"All right, I agree to get crucified", remarked Rex.

"Come on, it is not so bad", said Carol.

They both entered the flower shop and Carol pulled up a bunch of white and orange lilies. She asked the shopkeeper to arrange it in form of a bouquet. While walking out of the shop, Carol handed over the bouquet to Rex and said, "now tell me, isn't it beautiful?"

"Yes, definitely it is, but my problem is that I am not at all used to all these girlish things", said Rex.

"This is not girlish. By the way, don't you have a sister. I thought you had one?"

"Yes, I have one younger sister," quickly answered Rex.

"She doesn't do these girlish things?" Asked Carol.

"Oh, she is quite a tomboy", replied Rex.

Suddenly Rex realised, that his hostel had arrived. He stopped in front of the main gate. After dropping Rex at the hostel, Carol speeded up to reach her home. There were many things on her mind. On reaching home, Carol had a brief conversation with her parents, following which she got to work. She had never been afraid of hard work. In fact, it was as if she was addicted to work; the more she worked, the stronger was the desire to work harder still. She could not imagine life without work. As long there was coffee and music she could work effortlessly for hours together. Music had become the part of her life since she was very young. Her mother used to tell her how she would remain glued to the television if there were some song coming on it, when she was just two years old. By the time she was 4-5 years old, people were surprised when she would sing the songs with the lyrics in place even though she could not really understand the meaning. While young, her mother had given her some music lessons to help refine her voice.

She had been working on that design since past 2 hours. It had now finally reached her level of expectation. She had always been a perfectionist, working diligently until the last speck of perfection. She was putting the last minute finishing touches in her design. She was so happy, now that the design had come out perfectly well. Now she decided to take a break from work. She had been working hard throughout the day. As she rose to open the window of her room to get in some fresh air inside, her eye caught hold of a tiny twinkling star in the sky. It was very tiny, merely a speck in the sky, but as it twinkled, it appeared to be saying something and smiling at her.

Then she had a sudden urge to call up Rex. She felt strange at the sudden urge, she could not understand the reason why she should call Rex. However, her urge was so strong that it overcame her willpower. Instinctively, she called up Rex on his mobile.

"Hello", it was Rex on the line.

As soon as Carol heard Rex's voice, not really knowing what to say, she froze.

"Who is it", asked Rex sternly.

"It's me, Carol", Carol replied meekly.

"Oh, it's you. That's a pleasant surprise. I hope everything is fine", said Rex with a concern in his voice.

"Yes, everything is fine", said Carol. "I just called you because I was stuck up in one of the designs and I thought you could help me," lied Carol.

"Have you eaten your dinner yet?" Carol asked Rex.

"Yes, I have. Have you had yours?" Rex asked back.

"Yes, I too have had," answered Carol.

"Okay, now tell me about the problem you are facing" Rex questioned Carol again.

"Actually, I have made a rough sketch, but I am not too sure if the client would like it or not", said Carol.

"Carol, if you have made it, I am sure it is good. I saw you at work today. You are really very hard-working."

Carol blushed upon hearing her praise from Rex. She had not expected it, but was certainly enjoying it. In fact, even Rex was enjoying it. Carol realised when her mother called her asking her to come and help her with some household tasks, saying that she had been on the phone for nearly one hour.

After keeping the phone down, Carol thought to herself, "how could I talk to Rex for nearly an hour when I really did not have anything much to say". She looked outside the window again. She saw the twinkling star again. It appeared to be smiling at her. Carol smiled back.

Rex was alone in his room. He started thinking about Carol. There was something about her, something in her voice; something in the way she laughed that fascinated Rex. Rex lay on the bed thinking about Carol. He looked at the flowers, which Carol had gifted him. He had placed the flower bouquet carefully on the table at the side of his bed. Rex realized that the flowers indeed looked very beautiful. He thought about Carol and the way she had worked with him during the day. Soon he was fast asleep.

"Submit to love faithfully and it gives a person joy.
It intoxicates, it envelops, it isolates.
It creates fragrance in the air, ardour from coldness,
It beautifies everything around it"

—*Leoš Janáček (1854-1928)*
Czechoslovakia

CHAPTER 3

Addiction

Rex and Carol kept working on the design of the building for many months. They used to spend almost the whole day together. Slowly their friendship was growing stronger day by day. Rex had also known David, Carol's father since long. Their meetings also gradually increased. Rex frequently started visiting Carol's house to meet David. They both would often go for long walks together. Carol repeatedly tried to listen to their conversations but she was never successful. Though she never approved of the growing friendship between Rex and her father David, she pretended as if she did not care.

Carol had considerably improved her designing and creative skills under Rex's expert guidance. She realized that architecture was much more than just deciding how a building would look like. There were many other practical parameters attached to it, which she was now learning. She wanted to learn as much as she could about the buildings. However, at the same time, she never wanted to leave her creativity or artistic skills. Money or profit did not really matter to her. Rex was however different, Carol had realised working with him. While he too was creative and had a lot of practical experience, he took architecture to be a business, which would help him earn money.

Though the client had approved Carol's preliminary designs, she was yet to submit her final designs. She really wanted them to be the best and out of the box. She had done as much research as was physically and mentally possible. This was the first project she had undertaken in her career and she really wanted it to be successful. Rex had been extremely helpful assisting her out with every small intricacy involved in the designing process.

While working together as their friendship grew, the number of hours they had been spending with each other also gradually increased. Both of them had started looking for small excuses so that they would be able to spend maximum possible amount of time with each other. For example, Carol would work for long hours at the site itself, instead of taking work home, which she knew would have been more comfortable. On the other hand, Rex would pretend that he couldn't find any other way to go back home except for the car ride given by Carol.

The day of final design submission ultimately arrived and she submitted the designs. Both Carol and Rex were eagerly waiting for the client's answer. It was late in night; Carol was just lying in bed listening to some music, when suddenly her mobile phone rang. She realized Rex was on the line. He wanted her to come out for a ride on his bike.

"Rex, it is 11 pm in the night, are you sure you want to go for a bike ride at this hour?" Carol asked Rex over the phone.

"Why not, let's go to the nearby coffee shop. I have heard that they serve excellent coffee", Rex cajoled Carol.

After much persuasion by Rex, Carol eventually agreed and said "Okay I will get ready and come out in 15 minutes. I was just about to sleep".

"Alright, I shall wait for you", answered Rex.

Soon they both went to the coffee shop and had some coffee. While coming out of the cafeteria, Carol told Rex, "I can't believe I am with you at this hour of the night that too without telling anyone at home".

"I also don't know, but tell me one thing, did you not like it?" asked Rex.

"I don't know. Actually I was thinking about Susan. She just met with an accident. I am not sure if she would be able to come for the performance. You know, we have a duet musical performance in the club on coming Sunday," Carol said.

"Carol, what are you talking about? I know you are a good singer and shall be giving a performance with Susan.

But this is not what we are discussing at the moment," Rex said with the pitch of his voice slightly raised.

"I am not sure if we shall be able to give the performance because Susan had met with an accident," Carol continued talking about Susan as if she had not heard Rex.

"Look Carol, I don't want to discuss Susan", said Rex trying to control his anger.

Carol absent-mindedly continued blabbering about Susan.

"Carol, stop," Rex shouted losing his patience. "This is not what you want to say. Your mind is somewhere else."

"No, I am very much here", Carol said defensively.

"No, you aren't. You have been uttering some kind of gibberish since last half-an-hour. We have been discussing about Susan. I don't even know her. In fact, I am hearing her name from you for the first time. I know, this is not what you want to say."

"What are you saying, Rex?" Carol asked sounding puzzled.

"Carol, I know you so well that I know what is in your mind", Rex said glancing at her with a smile, all his anger had now disappeared.

"Okay, so tell me what is in my mind", asked Carol with authority directly looking in his eyes.

"You are addicted to me, aren't you?" Rex said, looking into Carol's eyes, holding her hand at the same time, the tone of his voice suddenly becoming soft.

So strong was his grip and so assertive was his voice that Carol could not resist him.

She meekly said, "No, that's not true".

"You know very well that it is true." "Don't lie to me, Carol. You know very well that you are addicted to me," Rex said with a chuckle. The word, 'addiction' had now become a joke for both of them.

Suddenly Carol realised that Rex was very close to her, he held her gently. Both their faces were nearly touching each other and they softly kissed each other. Carol had never felt this special ever before in her life. She felt as if everything around her had suddenly changed and had become better. She knew that she had certainly got addicted to Rex.

Soon afterwards, hiding her feelings while climbing his bike, Carol pretended as if nothing had happened. She simply told Rex, "Rex, it is time for us to go home".

She waved him goodbye carrying sweet memories of their first kiss.

Rex too was dizzy and felt lightheaded with excitement while going back home.

Carol walked inside her house, thinking about Rex. When she entered the house, she realized that her parents were fast asleep. It appeared that neither of them had sensed her absence. As she lay on the bed, trying to sleep she realized that she might not be able to meet Rex the next day. She had to help her mother organize a music show at the local club. She sent a text message to Rex on phone stating that she may not be able to meet him the next day. She might be able to give him a call in the evening. Carol did not realize when she went off to sleep. When she woke up in the morning, she recognized that she had a long day ahead. She wanted the day to end soon because she knew she would not be able to meet Rex. She wished that at least she gets a chance to speak to Rex when she comes back in the evening.

*"Three grand essentials to happiness in this life
are something to do, something to love
and something to hope for"*

—*Joseph Addison (1672-1719), England*

CHAPTER 4

Beautiful Life

After reaching home in the evening, Carol was on cloud nine. She tried to recall the incidence that had occurred last evening. She clearly knew that she was attracted towards Rex. Not only he was adorably funny and warm, he also understood her quite well. Since she had known Rex, simple things in life had started giving her more joy than ever before. She tried to recall his kiss. She was not sure why she did not react to it. All she could think was that it was indeed a magical moment. His kiss held divine madness akin to some kind of mystical dream. All of this appeared magical to Carol and she did not want to get out of it.

"Dinner is ready, Carol," Carol's thoughts were suddenly interrupted by her mother's voice; she was calling her to come to the dinner table.

Carol quietly sat at the dinner table quickly gulping her meals. Carol hardly uttered even a word while having her food. She wanted to get back to her magic world and think about Rex. After finishing her dinner, Carol rushed to her room. She wanted to talk to Rex on phone. She had missed talking to him the whole day today. On picking up the phone, she realized there were already several missed calls on it. It was Rex. He had been trying to talk to her. She immediately called him.

"You were trying to call me?" Carol asked as soon as Rex picked up his phone.

"Yes, I just wanted to tell you that you certainly are addicted to me", quipped in Rex.

"Why do you say so?" asked Carol.

"Because you never resisted when I kissed you. Now say, no", Rex teased Carol.

"No, yes . . ." muttered Carol. "I did not resist because there is something mysterious about you, which charms me, but I am not addicted to you."

"Oh yes, you are", Rex teased Carol again.

"Talk about yourself, Rex," Carol said. "I think it is the other way round. I think you are addicted to me."

"No, I am not," said Rex.

"Neither am I," joined in Carol.

Deliberately hiding each other's feelings, they both disconnected the phone.

While Carol lay on the bed, she was thinking only about Rex. "Today I shall dream about you, only you," she whispered to herself. She was soon asleep.

It was the vibrations of her phone, which had woke her up. She was still half asleep. With difficulty she opened up her eyes to check the time. It was 2 am in the morning. She was cursing the person who wanted to talk to her in the wee hours of morning. With sleepy eyes she looked at her phone. All her sleep and drowsiness disappeared as she saw Rex's name flashing on the screen of her phone.

"What happened, Rex?" Carol demanded. "Why are you calling me at such an hour?"

"I was unable to sleep, Carol. I was looking out of the window of my room and I could see a tiny star twinkling and smiling at me. It reminded me of you so I decided to call you. Also, I want to confess that I have become addicted to you and I cannot think about spending the rest of my life without you," Rex said it all in one go.

"Rex, I have known that since long, I was just waiting for you to say that", Carol said with a smile even though she realized that Rex could not see her.

"But you said you are not addicted to me", Rex told her.

"Don't tell me you believed that," quickly said Carol.

"No, I never believed you", Rex answered quietly.

"Then, what is your problem?" asked Carol.

"Nothing, we are both addicted to each other." Rex simply replied.

"Yes", said Carol with a sigh.

"You will not forget it later in the morning?" quipped Rex.

"No, I shall not forget it all my life", Carol replied.

"So, shall we meet today?" asked Rex.

"Definitely, only if you let me sleep. Can I sleep now?" Carol asked back.

"Would you be able to sleep now? I don't think I would be able to sleep today. I would be thinking about you only," said Rex.

"That's your problem. At least let me sleep", replied Carol.

"Okay sweetheart, you sleep", Rex replied.

After they both had disconnected the phone, Carol realized that she still wanted to speak to Rex. She was completely awake by now. She walked towards the window of her room. She tried to look towards the sky, searching for the star, which Rex had described. She saw several stars, which were shining brightly. However, she was unable to trace the one, which Rex had described.

She smiled at herself, thinking about Rex. She still could not believe that he had actually proposed her. She also could not believe that she had given him such a cold reaction. She wondered what Rex must have been thinking? Though Carol kept lying on her bed throughout after having spoken to Rex, she could not sleep for even one second.

Even though she had been awake the whole night after 2 am, Carol got up from the bed at her usual time in the morning. She gazed out of the window of her room. It was the same sky and the same trees as were yesterday. However, today they appeared special. Even the wind that was blowing and the birds that were chirping appeared different today. Everything appeared special because of Rex, she realised. She thought about him and smiled at herself. Though she had been meeting Rex every day since last 6 months, she desperately wanted to meet him today. Though not the type of person who believed in putting a lot of make-up or taking extra efforts while dressing up, today Carol really wanted to look her best. She chose a white silk dress from her closet. She quickly got ready. She quickly wanted to reach the construction site and meet Rex.

As soon as she saw Rex, she wanted to give him a tight hug. She realized that even Rex was wearing the best of his clothes. He was wearing a maroon coloured shirt, the colour which both of them particularly liked. She wanted to run to him. However, today many people were present. Moreover, Rex was busy entertaining one person after the other. Both Rex and Carol could not get to spend a single moment in privacy throughout the day.

It was late evening, time to leave. Still Carol had not got any chance to approach Rex. Throughout the day, Rex had been surrounded by people.

Gloomily Carol sat on the worktable. She tried to complete some unfinished design. Softly, she cursed "Rex, silly man, he could not have found some time, not even 5 minutes for me today?"

To keep Rex off her mind, she kept on working. She had decided that she would also not make the first move today.

Carol was engrossed in her work, when suddenly she received the notification of a text message on her mobile phone. She checked it; it was a "missing you" message from Rex. She read it and smiled at herself. She replied back on the text message, "me too".

"Come outside", instantly came Rex's reply via text message.

Carol quickly winded up her work and went outside. As she was waiting outside looking for Rex, she realized somebody was pulling her arm. It was Rex grabbing her arm. Before she could react, he said, "Run with me before they catch hold of me to finish off my pending work." They both ran together towards Carol's car. Rex hurriedly snatched the car keys from Carol's hand and sat down on the driver's seat. He told Carol, "Come on sit inside, fast."

"I thought it was my car", said Carol.

"That's right, it was your car, now it's our car", replied Rex.

"Yes it is", said Carol sweetly as she held his hand.

"Madam, if you hold my hand, how will I change gears. There surely would be an accident and we both shall die," Rex told Carol when she continued to hold his hand while he was trying to change the gears.

"I don't care as long as I am with you," Carol replied.

"From now onwards, you can always be sure that you shall never be alone. There always would be someone besides you to take your care", whispered Rex softly in her ear.

"Anyways, where are you taking me?" asked Carol changing the topic.

"To my hostel room," Rex told her.

"What will I do there?" Carol asked slightly perplexed.

"You shall find out soon," Rex replied nonchalantly.

Soon they reached Rex's bachelor accommodation. Rex let her inside the hostel.

As Rex showed her the way, they both walked down till his room.

Rex opened the door of his room and ushered her inside after covering her eyes with his hand.

"What are you doing, Rex?" Carol questioned Rex.

"I have a surprise for you," answered Rex.

When Rex removed his hand from her eyes Carol could not believe what she saw. He had let her in a small room meant for a single person. The whole room was dimly lit. At least a dozen of bouquets were symmetrically placed in the centre. In between these bouquets there were lit candles placed on beautiful candle stands. A beautiful fragrance was coming from the room.

"This room of yours, Rex, it looks beautiful, when did you get time to do all this?" Carol asked with a smile on her face.

"I got it done through a friend, while we were working at the office" Rex replied.

"So you had been pretending to be busy all day", Carol said.

"Yes, said Rex with a timid smile. I wanted to make this day special for you", Rex said holding Carol in his arms.

While in his embrace, Carol saw an enlarged photograph of Rex and herself plastered on the wall.

"Rex, when did you take this photograph?" Carol quizzed him.

"Some day when you were wearing this same white dress and looking as beautiful as you are looking today", replied Rex.

"So you had been noticing me since so long", asked Carol.

"Yes definitely", quickly replied Rex. "Now, I am totally addicted to you."

"Ditto", spontaneously replied Carol.

"No, don't use that word", instantly said Rex.

"Why? Ditto implies that I mean the same as you," Carol asked inquisitively.

"I know Carol what ditto means. Just don't say that, it reminds me of someone", said Rex in an irritated tone.

"Who is that someone? Please tell me", Carol cajoled Rex.

"It reminds me of Jane", said Rex thoughtfully after a few minutes of persuasion by Carol.

"Who is Jane?" Carol questioned immediately.

"Jane was with me in college during my graduation. We both were deeply in love. Those were very beautiful days", Rex sighed.

"Then why is she not with you today?" Carol asked sounding disturbed.

Rex did not speak. He was just staring blankly at the wall.

"Rex, it is alright if you don't want to tell me," said Carol while gently caressing Rex.

"Look Carol, I don't want to hide anything from you, especially not today when we are making a new beginning. Jane is no more with us. She died because she developed cancer in her brain. They operated her, but could not save her and I lost my Jane 6 years back", Rex said with sadness clearly written over his face.

Rex suddenly slumped on the chair. Carol held his hand and tried to comfort him.

"After Jane's death, it was very difficult for me. Her death brought me to a point of extreme destruction. I went into self-isolation. I withdrew myself from the world and had built a wall around myself. At one point of time, I wanted to commit suicide. Somehow I took control of my life. But, I had never thought that anyone, especially a girl could penetrate that wall. And then you came along. You completely destroyed that wall. You did not destroy it by removing brick by brick. You simply came out of nowhere and blew it into pieces," Rex told Carol, holding her in his arms.

"Rex, all this must have been so difficult for you," said Carol.

"Yes, it was difficult for me, but you managed to seduce me", commented Rex while smiling mischievously at Carol.

"No, I never enticed you," replied Carol making a face at Rex.

"Carol, don't be upset. Look, I have got something for you. Come on, look." Rex said, taking out a small beautiful box out of his pocket.

Carol still showing her fake anger said, "Rex, I don't want any more of your surprises. Throw it out of the window. As far as I am concerned, I just want to go home."

"Are you sure you want me to throw this?" Rex asked.

"Yes, please throw it," Carol said without even taking a look at the gift.

"Are you sure you want me to throw away this beautiful diamond ring," Rex asked. "I am asking you for the last time," Rex asked Carol while thrusting the opened box towards her.

"Ring . . . .", Carol suddenly stammered, "Rex, what are you talking about? You have got me a ring?"

"Yes, I thought you liked diamonds. We can throw it away if you want. Just that it costed me a small fortune." Rex replied, trying to sound as casual as possible.

"Why a ring?" Carol asked trying hard to hide her excitement.

"Because I want you to be Mrs Carol Harrison from being Miss Carol Wilde", replied Rex. "Now please don't irritate me. Obviously I want to marry you. Give me your hand so that I can put the ring on your finger."

"Rex, you never cease to surprise me. When did you get this ring?" Carol fondly asked Rex, while he was putting the ring on her finger.

"I bought it many days back and wanted to give to you. Just that I was not able to discover your true feelings about me. Even though I was pretty sure that you had become addicted to me, I wanted to be sure," said Rex again giving Carol a mischievous look.

"Now you know", Carol solemnly asked.

"Yes and I also know that we both are fatally addicted to each other. I love you and want to marry you", Rex said placing the ring on Carol's finger.

"I love you too and I shall certainly marry you", Carol said, giving Rex a tight hug.

Rex and Carol soon got married and shifted in an apartment, which Rex had rented. The first day when Rex showed Carol the apartment, she loved it.

"Rex, I love it, but it is a semi-furnished house," Carol said.

"I have already hired an interior designer to work on it," Rex had told her.

"Who?" she had asked with excitement.

"You, and she had agreed to work for free," Rex giggled.

"Now, who has told you that?" Carol said showing her fake anger.

"Your eyes", Rex had said gently kissing her on her cheek.

Carol's first architectural assignment had been really successful. Now, she decided to take a break for few months from her office so that she could manage the household. Little did Carol realize at that time that this was meant to be her last architectural assignment.

That night Carol said a small prayer to thank God for her blissful life. She gazed out of the window to look at a twinkling star. Sadly today, it did not appear to be twinkling with a smile. Instead it appeared to be rather gloomy and frightened. It was scary.

"I am being a pessimistic fool", thought Carol as she went to put off the lights of her room and soon went to sleep in Rex's arms.

"Life is a series of collisions with the future;
It is not the sum of what we have been, but
what we yearn to be"

—*Jose Ortega Y Gasset (1883-1955), Spain*

CHAPTER 5

Something is Wrong

As Carol got up in the morning, she experienced a slight tingling sensation on her fingers. As she rose from bed, she remembered waking up several times last night because of the strange tingling sensation on her fingers. She thought that she would share this with Rex. She started calling out for Rex. However, he was not there; he had already left for office. She realized that he had left without telling her. Initially during the first few weeks of marriage, he would always bid her goodbye before leaving home. She wondered why Rex had changed suddenly after marriage. In her turmoil, she forgot about the tingling sensation in the hands. She got up from her bed and continued with her normal household chores. As usual, nothing eventful occurred throughout the day. She called up her mother and spoke to her. She also called up a few friends asking them to look for a probable vacancy of an architect at their work place. Carol had now become tired of listening to their comments, "your husband and father, both are big architects and you are asking us to look for a job for you? Is this some kind of joke?" her friends would often tell her. She would just keep quiet, silently listening to their comments because she did not want to gain any sympathy from them by telling them about her problem.

In the afternoon Carol lied down to take a nap and started thinking about those good old days with Rex. They were not many. Still she tried to remember those days just to make herself feel happy. Suddenly Carol woke up due to some noise. As she woke up she realized that the phone was ringing out loud. When she tried to run towards the phone to grab it, she suddenly felt a strange pang in her back. "Am I getting too old?" thought Carol with a smile on her face. Probably some muscle in the back has cramped due to my sudden actions. It was Rex on the phone, "why did you take so long to pick up my phone?" She had become used to this. Rex had now started nagging her for even the smallest and tiniest of things.

"I think I am getting old," said Carol with a chuckle, thinking that Rex would laugh with her too.

"Listen Carol, I don't have much time to waste. I shall be coming late for the dinner today," Rex retorted back.

"Okay, but you had left early in the morning too because when I woke up you were not there, where were you?" politely asked Carol.

"You need not worry about that", said Rex rather rudely as he snapped down the phone.

Carol again became sad. This was not the first time he had been doing this. This had become his routine thing over the past few months. She could not even remember the last time they happily enjoyed a meal together. She suddenly realized the tingling in her fingers. It had not disappeared as Carol had earlier thought that it would. In fact it had rather become more intense.

"Am I about to fall sick?" questioned Carol to herself. "I would discuss it with Rex today."

A few months had passed since her marriage. The fairy-tale life she had dreamt about had ended long ago. Her life was not what she had thought it to be. Soon after her marriage, David's interference in her life had suddenly increased. Every other day either Rex would be visiting David's office or David would be visiting their house. Carol had not approved the growing friendship between David and Rex even prior to their marriage. Following her marriage, she had never thought that their friendship would grow to such an extent. Though Carol tried to patiently control her anger most of the times, at times she would show her disapproval openly to Rex. Rex had strongly told her, "Besides being my father-in-law, David is also my mentor and guide. I did my first job under him. So don't ever expect me to break my relationship with him."

Carol would often tell Rex, "You have been very well aware all this time that unfortunately my relationship with my father had never been the way it should have been; you are well aware of the problems my mother and myself had to undergo because of him."

"Yes, I know that very well Carol, but my relationship with David is on the professional front. It is at a different level altogether," Rex would say.

Carol tried to divert her mind from all this. As it is, she already had several arguments with Rex because of David. She tried to think of something else by watching some sitcom on the television. However her mind soon drifted back to Rex. She started thinking how Rex had come back one day from office and informed her about an important matter without even consulting her.

"I have left my job at the Planners and Designers firm," Rex had announced.

Carol felt sad at Rex's announcement because she had many memories attached with her first assignment at the Planners and Designers firm. This was the place where she had first met Rex.

"You took such a big decision and not even once discussed it with me," surprised by Rex's hasty decision, Carol immediately questioned Rex.

"Carol, it was not a hasty decision, rather a well-planned career move. Anyway, I had already discussed it with David", casually replied Rex.

"You discussed it with David and you did not think it was important to at least let me know about your decision?" asked Carol.

"I have entered into 50/50 partnership with David. Now I don't have to work under someone else. I can be my own boss. David is a nice person. I don't know why you do not like him. He has even changed the name of his firm from D&W to D&R, which stands for David and Rex," Rex said with a note of excitement in his voice.

"What about my job Rex? I had been working under you. Now where will I work?" suddenly gripped with fear, Carol asked Rex.

"Why do you need to work Carol? Now, I am there to earn for both of us. You need not work, David has also promised to gift us a bigger apartment. And it shall be bigger than this one, where I also will not have to pay the rent," Rex said trying to calm Carol.

"Rex, you know I don't work to earn money. I like doing it. Architecture is my passion," Carol impatiently replied.

"So, what is the problem? I am not asking you to stop working. You can join me in David's office", calmly said Rex.

"You very well know I would never join David's office, I don't like taking favours from him," replied Carol.

"That's your problem, I have not stopped you," Rex said ending the discussion by leaving the room.

Carol even now could not believe what Rex had said at that time.

"He had been so supportive of my professional career prior to marriage. Now, he appears to be totally oblivious about my passion or career," sadly thought Carol.

Carol had tried many a times to mould herself into doing the household chores and not really worrying too much about her career. However, the ambitious drive in her would appear sooner or later.

"Now that my first assignment in architectural had been successful, I might get a new Job elsewhere. Meanwhile, I should concentrate on improving my previous designs and making the new ones," Carol would often think trying to console herself.

Nonetheless her gloominess would return soon. She could not imagine that Rex had teamed up with David and completely ignored her feelings about her father. With Rex joining up with David, her relationship with David had strained up even further. To make herself feel cheerful, today she planned out an elaborate dinner for Rex.

Rex had come quite late in the night and had snapped her immediately for wasting so much money on an elaborate meal when he was not even feeling hungry. He had slept that night without even having one bite. Carol was very sad and cried away, while she could hear Rex snoring.

"At least one of us is getting a sound sleep", thought Carol as eventually she too slept away.

When Carol woke up next morning she realized that it was difficult to get up from the bed. The pain in her back had worsened and now it was also involving her belly. Carol then thought, "What about the tingling sensation, do I still have it?"

She decided to check. No, there was no tingling. Instead it had been replaced by a strange numbness. "I think it is all in my mind. This is nothing but psychological", Carol tried to convince herself.

Again as she looked around Rex was not there in the house. As she got up with a heavy heart, she again started thinking about Rex. "No, I would not think about him. I suppose it's just that I have become crazy staying around in the house. I believe I should divert my mind towards something more productive," Carol tried to console herself.

After having Kellogg's with milk, she took out her sketchbooks and other stationery. She realized that it was difficult for her just to bring those things to the table, when the distance would have been just about some 10-15 steps. She had been observing similar weakness since past few days when she had noticed that it required her to put enormous amount of strength in doing normal household chores. She just realized that this morning itself she had difficulty in taking out a litre of milk from the refrigerator. She had dismissed the thought thinking it to be merely psychological but now she noticed that she was having difficulty in lifting books and stationery items as well. She even faced difficulty in drawing sketches in her sketchbook. "Now, this cannot be psychological. This is very much real," thought Carol feeling a little scared. She immediately called up Rex on his mobile phone. Until now she really had not got an opportunity to discuss her symptoms with Rex. In fact, she herself had avoided bringing up the problem in front of Rex.

"He already has so much in his mind to handle; I must not bother him further. Besides, this appears to more psychological rather than result of some disease," Carol had previously often consoled herself.

Her thoughts were interrupted with a "hello"; it was Rex on the phone. "What has happened Carol? Why are you bothering me, don't you know I am working," shouted Rex over the phone. Carol suddenly did not know what to say as she realized that she had also been having difficulty in holding the receiver of the phone. "Rex," she silently said, I think I am sick . . . ."

"So why are you calling me?" thundered Rex, "Go see a doctor, call a taxi."

Carol weakly said, "yes I shall do that, but can you come?"

"You reach the doctor's clinic, I will come there directly", replied Rex with his voice suddenly becoming soft.

"Okay", said Carol.

Carol also experienced difficulty while changing her dress. It took her nearly three times more time than usual, when she just was trying to wear a long, one-piece dress. As she started buttoning her jacket, she realized that it was impossible for her to do that today.

After fixing up an appointment with the family physician, Dr George, she called a cab. She noticed that she became breathless just after climbing 5 stairs. "What is wrong with me?" Carol tried to contemplate as she boarded the taxi. She felt a little relieved thinking, "At least Rex would be coming to the doctor's clinic. He still cares for me. It's just me who thinks so much and is unnecessarily making a mountain of the mole hill."

As she reached the doctor's clinic, she realized that Rex was not there. She sat down in the waiting area hoping for her turn to come soon. As she flipped through the pages of some magazine lying on the table, she realized that it was getting progressively difficult for her to flip the pages. Suddenly she heard a voice.

"Is that Mrs Carol Harrison?" That was the nurse calling out her name.

"Yes, that's me," said Carol suddenly getting up. As she got up suddenly the pain in her belly and back appeared to be getting stronger. She forced herself towards Dr George's room. Rex had yet not come. Now, she realized that she had been really missing him and desperately wished he was there. She walked inside the doctor's room. Dr George was almost like a family friend, so they were familiar with each other. "Where is Rex? Dr George asked Carol.

"I am here", said Rex, suddenly arriving on the door, panting. Though it was still fall and winters had not yet arrived, nevertheless, the weather was quite cold. Still, there was Rex standing at the door half drenched in sweat. "I am sorry, I got a little late because of some work", Rex quickly replied looking at the perplexed expression on George's face.

Carol's pale face lit up on seeing Rex.

Dr George started taking history of her clinical complaints, while a nurse assisting him quickly kept jotting those points on a note pad.

"You mean to say the problem started with a tingling sensation in your fingers, since past 3-4 weeks?" George questioned Carol.

"Yes, it kept increasing in severity. In the beginning, I thought that it is just my speculation and it would go away on its own. Initially the sensation would often change. Sometimes it felt like burning. Some other times it felt as if someone was tickling me. Sometimes it would feel as if someone is pricking me and some other time that peculiar tingling sensation would return again. Then this feeling turned into numbness. I also started experiencing some trouble while doing normal household chores, especially when I would use my hands. For instance I started having trouble taking out small things like the milk carton from the refrigerator. Now, I take nearly twice to thrice the time more as compared to what I used to previously take while performing simple tasks. I just noticed while sitting in your office that I also have problem in flipping pages of the magazine," Carol replied.

"You had never told me about this before", Rex asked Carol.

"I kept ignoring the symptoms thinking it was just my imagination and would pass off on its own. It was only today I felt that I could be really sick," Carol answered.

"Do you have problems while writing also?" George enquired.

"Yes, that too I noticed today while trying to draw a design in my sketch book. I am unable to draw a single straight line. Besides I also have to put in double the effort," replied Carol.

"Are you also having trouble while walking?" asked George again.

"Not exactly, but I am having this weird nagging pain both in my back and belly since past few days," replied Carol.

"Was this in anyway related to your numbness?" George asked.

"Yes, I think both symptoms started almost together. I don't seem to remember which one came first and which one came next," Carol answered.

"What is wrong doctor?" interrupted Rex. He now genuinely sounded worried.

"I am not too sure Rex," replied George, "Let me examine her first".

Dr George took Carol into the examination room. After nearly half an hour, the doctor walked out of the examination room into his office.

Rex was sitting on the chair in the doctor's office, wearing a worried expression on his face. When he saw George, he stood up from his chair.

"Is she fine, George?" Rex asked impatiently.

"I hope she be fine," George quietly replied.

"Why, what's wrong with her?" interrogated Rex.

"I think a neurologist must examine her," answered George.

"Why a neurologist, George?" Rex asked looking worried.

"A neurologist, because I think she has something more severe than we can imagine. While examining her, I have realized that she has demonstrable weakness in both her upper extremities. Sensations of the hand and forearm have also been affected on both the sides. Bladder and bowel functions and her legs have so far not been affected. I am not sure about the cause of all this. I think we would need an MRI or a CT scan, whatever the neurologist says. I think better idea would be calling a neurologist here and taking his opinion."

"What have you told her?" Rex asked George.

"Nothing, I just examined her and then came out to tell you my thoughts," replied George.

As Rex saw the nurse taking Carol out of the examination room, he suddenly jumped from his chair and quickly walked towards her.

He realized that suddenly she was looking very frail. He held her hand and whispered in her ear, "Carol, don't worry everything shall be fine."

Carol held his hand very tight and asked him, "Rex what is wrong with me?"

Rex coolly replied, "Nothing, you shall be fine soon. George has called a neurologist, Dr William Humphreys."

"Neurologist!, why, Rex?" Carol asked sounding slightly tensed.

"Because George just wants to be sure that you are absolutely fine", replied Rex, gently caressing her face.

In a short the neurologist, Dr William Humphreys was there and he again examined Carol. He suggested an MRI examination for confirmation of the diagnosis. Meanwhile, arrangements were being made to admit Carol to the hospital.

"We should always be mindful of the ever-present prospect of death, and never forget it for an instant.

If we do so, the distractions of the world will not infect us and it shall be easier for us to follow our path in the earnest."

—*Yoshida Kenko (1283-c. 1351), Japan*

CHAPTER 6

Everything is Wrong

It was completely dark and there was a shrill sound. Carol closed her eyes and started thinking. Though she could not think clearly, she vaguely remembered being brought to a tube-like structure in a wheel chair. She remembered Rex accompanying her and holding her hand. Other medical staff had also been accompanying them. Dr Humphreys had already warned Carol about the shrill, clanging sounds she may hear inside the MRI machine.

"Those sounds are the result of giant magnets in the MRI machine", Carol recalled Dr Humphreys telling her. He had comforted her saying that she would be laying inside the tube for approximately half an hour to 45 minutes. Now, she just remembered the darkness inside the tube.

When she did see some light, she realized that she was no longer in that tube, she was in the ward. Rex was sitting on the chair next to her bed. "I was in that tube, what happened, what am I doing here?" She asked Rex.

"You fell asleep at the time of examination. MRI examination is over," Rex answered.

"What is the result?" Carol asked quickly.

"You don't worry about it, you shall be fine soon," said Rex trying to hide the anxiousness in his voice.

"What is wrong with me?" She held Rex's hand and tried to squeeze it hard. However, she was unable to do it. She then noticed a tube attached to her hand.

"Look I know something is seriously wrong. Otherwise why is this tube attached to my hand," asked Carol firmly.

"The tube is for injecting the medicines directly inside your veins", patiently replied Rex.

"Medicines through veins, I must be terribly sick, Rex", sadly said Carol.

"The doctor has said that the weakness in your arms and hand is the result of some infection of the nerve cells", said Rex while holding her hand. "They are giving you steroids to fight with that infection. You shall be fine after the infection has been removed," Rex added while looking at Carol with a smile. He realized that she was not listening to him and had already gone to sleep.

He released his hand from her grip and sat on the chair looking outside the window with a vacant expression in his eyes. He remembered Dr Humphreys calling him to discuss Carol's MRI report. Dr Humphreys had explained to Rex that the results of the MRI examination pointed towards a lesion in her spine.

Dr Humphreys had told Rex, "To be more precise, I think Carol is most likely suffering from a neurological disorder, Transverse myelitis".

Rex was speechless! He fumbled for words. He had heard the name of this illness for the first time in his life.

Dr Humphreys, quickly understanding that Rex might not be aware of this illness quickly explained, "Transverse myelitis is a neurological disorder caused by soreness of the spinal cord due to some kind of infection. Spinal cord is the bundle of nervous tissue extending towards the backbone from the brain. Attacks of infection can damage the nerve cell fibres, resulting in dysfunction of nervous system and loss of function of the spinal cord. Symptoms gradually occur over several hours to several weeks."

Dr Humphreys had warned Rex that Carol's condition might further worsen over the coming few days. Paresis may spread to her legs as well and may increase in intensity. And there might be some disturbances in passing urine or stools. "Some amount of urinary or faecal incontinence is also possible," Dr Humphreys had told Rex.

"Will she ever get fine?" Rex remembered asking Dr Humphreys.

"Rex, it is difficult to say anything at present. We still need to get a few more tests done to confirm the diagnosis of transverse myelitis. Some degree of disability is likely to persist in approximately 40 per cent of cases even after the completion of treatment. There is a likelihood of being left with permanent physical disabilities. Recovery may begin anytime within 2 to 12 weeks of the onset of symptoms and may continue for up to 2 years. Only about one-third of people affected with transverse myelitis are able to obtain full recovery from their symptoms. The remaining people may show either incomplete recovery or no recovery at all. But Rex you need not worry at all because Carol is young and younger patients are likely to have a complete recovery", Dr Humphreys tried to assure Rex.

"What kind of tests would you do?" asked Rex not really knowing what to say.

"Some blood tests and a lumbar puncture," Dr Humphreys answered quickly.

"What is lumbar puncture?" Rex asked sounding worried and confused.

"Lumbar puncture is a simple test in which a long needle is inserted through the spine into the spinal cord. A small amount of fluid is drained out, which has composition similar to the brain fluid. Analysis of this fluid gives information related to infection in the brain," explained Dr Humphreys.

Rex remembered Dr Humphreys saying, "There is presently no effective cure for people with transverse myelitis. Treatments are planned to help and improve patients' symptoms. We shall also be prescribing her steroids during the first few weeks to reduce the amount of soreness and infection. Painkillers shall take care of her pain."

"However, the most important aspect of treatment would begin later once she gets a little stable. This phase of treatment comprises of keeping the patient's body functioning while hoping for either complete or partial spontaneous recovery of the nervous system and would include physical as well as rehabilitative therapy. Physical therapy would help improve her muscle strength, coordination, and range of motion. Rehabilitative therapy would teach her various strategies for carrying out activities of daily living such as bathing, dressing and performing household tasks in new ways in order to overcome or compensate for her disabilities in case there is any. Both rehabilitation and physical therapy can help people with physical limitation to become as functionally independent as possible and thereby attain the best possible quality of life." Dr Humphreys had patiently explained the entire management plan to Rex.

Rex's thoughts were suddenly interrupted by Dr George tapping on his shoulder. A nurse was trying to wake up Carol while George told Rex that they required performing a lumbar puncture on Carol.

Soon after the lumbar puncture was performed, a team of senior doctors arrived to examine Carol. After examining her they explained to both of them a little about transverse myelitis, following which they asked both of them if they had any questions.

Carol had just one question, which she asked, "Doctor, will I ever get alright?"

"Look Carol, you are getting one of the best treatments in this world. Rest everything, time will tell. You might eventually have a 100% recovery," Dr Humphreys replied.

Soon after the team of doctors left, Rex also told Carol that he would quickly come after having a hurried bite in the hospital cafeteria.

By now, Carol was wide-awake. She could not make out complete sense of the medical jargon, which the doctors had said, but by instinct she knew that this was a long-term sickness and she might have to stay in the hospital for a long time. She did not want to think about it. At least not know, when Rex was being nice and caring to her. She thought about the way he had held her hand while taking her for the MRI examination. Even though she knew that sickness was not a nice thing, but she felt it to be a blessing in disguise because it brought her close to Rex. She tried feeling blessed by looking at some twinkling star. She asked the nurse to open the window of her room.

As the nurse opened the window, Carol tried to gaze outside. However, it being a cloudy night she could trace none. But, she herself had realized the strength of her love for Rex. She felt asleep again thinking about Rex.

Carol was walking with Rex towards the office holding his hand and she could even feel his grip properly today. They both were enjoying working together. She was making some very elaborate design for a building and he was guiding her, just like those good old days. Suddenly, someone asked her to come for dinner. She said that she was not hungry yet and would have it later. However, the voice continued to call her for dinner. Soon she also felt someone tapping on her shoulder. As she tried to resist with her arms, she suddenly realized that she was having difficulty in moving them. It was becoming difficult for her to resist the hand, which continued to tap over her shoulder. Suddenly she heard the voice getting louder. It was the nurse. She was trying to wake her up. Carol woke up with a startle.

Carol was disappointed to get up. Rex was not there. The good old days were not back, she realized with a lump in her throat.

"Hi I am Daisy. I am the nurse who shall be looking after you," said Daisy, a middle-aged woman with gray hair. Her face with wrinkles appeared to reflect the compassion and experience she had in her heart.

Carol smiled faintly at her. She was happy to see Daisy and had taken an instant liking for the old lady.

"Your dinner is ready. I have placed it on the table attached to your bed. If you need any help just press the buzzer and I shall come," Daisy told Carol gently.

"Why would I require help?" thought Carol. The extent and severity of her sickness had yet not completely stuck her.

Diverting her thoughts about her sickness, Carol tried to think about food. She realized now that she hadn't eaten anything since morning. Not that she was hungry; just to divert her mind, Carol tried to jump towards the food table. However, she winced in pain as she tried to do so. Her back was really hurting bad and she was feeling very weak. Now, she realized that she was ill. There was some discomfortable feeling coming from within which made her quite restless. She started eating the food. Though she was not too sure if she would like the hospital food, it actually smelt nice.

"What is it?" Carol asked her nurse Daisy.

"It is a quiche with spinach and cheese," Daisy replied.

"What's a quiche?" Carol asked deliberately trying to irritate Daisy.

"Quiche is a quiche. I don't know how to explain it further," Daisy said, losing her patience slightly.

The quiche, not only looked good, it smelt good as well, so she decided to try it out.

As Carol tried to dig in the spoon, she recognized it was difficult for her to do so. She realized her weakness was getting worse. It was impossible for her to cut out a piece. Putting it in her mouth would be impossible too, she apprehended.

Now she knew why Daisy was showing her readiness to help her. She would require Daisy's help in almost every small thing she would need to do.

"Daisy, I am unable to eat this", Carol said with tears in her eyes. "Please help me".

"Carol, don't worry. Darling, I would be always there to help you. Just relax. Rest your back against the pillow. You shall feel less pain. You are like my daughter, I shall feed you. Just open your mouth," said Daisy while putting a spoonful of quiche in Carol's mouth.

"Where is Rex, my husband?" Carol asked.

"He said he had some urgent work," Daisy replied, "You were sleeping, he never wanted to disturb you. So he gave us his contact number and left saying that he would be back soon. But don't worry, your mother Judy called up at the nursing station to say that she would be visiting you today."

While Carol was eating her meal, she again started thinking about Rex. She wondered what important work Rex had. She again started thinking about Rex and the way he had held her hand. She, however felt happy that she would be meeting her mother. Judy had been regularly visiting Carol ever since she had been admitted in the hospital.

Daisy opened the window of Carol's room. Strong breeze was blowing outside which brushed past the curtains leaving the window wide open. There were no stars in the sky today.

After having her meal Carol slept off. In the evening when Carol woke up she saw her mother sitting on the sofa in her room, smiling at her. It was always a joy for Carol to see her mother. Judy told Carol that Rex had been frequently visiting their place in the past month to meet David. "They both have long discussions, but I am not really sure what they talk about," Judy said sounding a little worried.

"Mom, they must be discussing something related to business," said Carol, trying to calm her mother.

Carol recalled that David had come to the hospital once, a few days back. She could not make out if he had come to meet her or Rex because he hardly spoke to her even for a few minutes. All the time, she had been discussing something with Rex.

Over the coming few days, Carol's illness came under the control of medications and other therapies initiated by the doctors. Nevertheless, her sickness caused her to remain admitted in the hospital and be confined to bed for nearly 6 months.

"Situations are easier to enter than to exit;

But it is only common sense to look for a way
out before venturing in"

—*Aesop (620-560 BC), Greece*

CHAPTER 7

Revelation

Today after staying in the hospital for nearly 4 months, Carol was discharged home. Though there had been a considerable improvement in her health, some residual disability in her hands still remained. She was thrilled to know that she would be going home. She was yet not sure about how she would manage alone at home, she was still very happy to leave hospital.

When she entered her house the first thing she noticed was that a large photograph of her and Rex, taken at the time of their wedding, was obviously missing from the wall of their living room. She remembered how both of them together had plastered that photograph on the front wall of their house.

"Rex where is our photograph which was stuck up on the wall here?" Carol inquisitively asked Rex.

"It is not required now," Rex said abruptly.

"Why?" enquired Carol quickly.

"Because now you are yourself here," Rex said with a sly smile on his face.

"But I was here previously as well", said Carol not at all convinced. "You had said that the photograph would always remain here till we are alive," said Carol softly.

"Till our relationship is alive", whispered Rex, almost to himself.

"Rex, you said something. Say again. I could not understand," replied Carol.

"It's nothing. You don't think about these things. You just concentrate on your health. I want you to be back to normal soon and start working," Rex answered.

She started looking around her. Everything else appeared to be the same, similar to how she had left it before going to the hospital.

She looked at the half-embroidered "Winne the Pooh", the Disney character lying on her bed. She had made it using cross-stitch embroidery work. She stared at with sadness because she knew that she might never be able to complete it now.

"I am not sure if the fine refined movements of your fingers would come back to normal ever again", Dr William Humphreys had told her at the time of her last examination.

However, Carol was sure that her fingers would never be able to come back to normal again. She could perform crude movements with her hand, like she could grasp various objects. However, it was impossible to do fine movements using her hands. She had learnt to live with that reality now. Initially, she had not realized the degree of disability this might cause. She had been undergoing continuous physiotherapy, which had enabled her to independently perform the tasks of daily living. Her back still ached and there was still some weakness. She was still being prescribed steroid preparations. She was facing side effects related to this as well. The steroids had caused her to gain a lot of weight. She was also experiencing severe mood swings. However, she was not bothered about all those things today. She was just happy to return home after so many days.

"After so many days I shall finally be with Rex in our house," mused Carol.

It had not even been 2 years past her marriage. But she did not want to think about any of that. She just wanted to enjoy the feeling of being at home after such a long time. She glanced throughout the room just to be sure that everything was in place. Suddenly, her eyes caught attention of the corner of the room, the place where the table was present. All her sketchbooks and other instruments for making the designs were present neatly piled up on the table, just the way she had left it. She could also see a half-open sketchbook with a half drawn design of a building. She remembered, this was the last one she had been making before she had become sick and had to be admitted to the hospital. She planned that after spending together some time with

Rex today, she would start working on the half-drawn sketches.

Even as Carol was thinking, she saw Rex getting dressed up to go out. He was putting on his jacket and wearing his shoes.

"Are you going somewhere?" She asked Rex.

"Yes, do you have some problem with that?" abruptly replied Rex.

"Not really, I had just come back from the hospital after 6 months. I thought I would get to spend some time with you today and I had been looking forward towards it since long."

"I have already spent a lot of time with you rather wasted time on you. Now I have other things in life which I also want to do," said Rex rather rudely as he forcefully opened the door, slammed it shut and left.

Carol sat on the bed shocked and heartbroken, with tears in her eyes. She realized that Rex had become worse than before. She had contemplated that Rex's behaviour might come back to normal when she would return home. She consoled herself by thinking that Rex's office work must have suffered a lot because he had to spend a lot of time in the hospital. There were many days when he would just not be there the whole day in the hospital. The nurses would often tell her that they tried tracing him at his office, but he had not even been there. She wondered where he went. She had tried to ask him a few times, but he never gave her any definite reply.

That day, Rex arrived home a few hours later. On being questioned by Carol regarding his whereabouts, he shouted at her again.

Suddenly there was a ring on the doorbell again. Rex yelled again at Carol for opening the door. Carol silently wiped her tears and opened the door. It was a courier boy, who handled her a parcel. She opened the packet and saw that there was a DVD of the movie, 'P.S. I love you', which Rex had ordered. She felt happy thinking that Rex had ordered the DVD for both of them.

Carol immediately went to the room where Rex was sitting and thanked him for the movie. She was bitterly surprised when he impolitely said, "which DVD? I never ordered any DVD for you."

"This is DVD of the film, P.S I love you, starring Hilary Swank and Gerard Butler", the movie we both wanted to see since a long time", Carol said in one breath.

"But I never ordered this for you, this is for Er . . . ." Rex abruptly stopped himself from saying anything further. He just snatched the DVD from her hands and walked out of the room.

Carol went emotionless for some time. She tried to divert her mind from thinking why Rex had ordered that DVD. She also tried to contemplate about what Rex had suddenly stopped himself from saying; something which he almost blurted out; she wondered what Er . . . stood for? Was there something which

Rex was hiding from her? Or was this all just her imagination? There were so many questions in her mind for which she had no answer . . . .

In order to divert her mind, she decided to do something productive. She sat on the table, the place from where she loved to work. She went to the other room to put on the music, which she always listened to while working. When she came back to the table to start working, she realized that this amount of little activity had also made her breathless. The disease, transverse myelitis, had taken a toll on her. She tried to avert her mind away from Rex by indulging in some kind of activity.

She struggled to draw a straight line on the sketchbook using a pencil and a ruler, but was unable to do so. Her fingers were too weak to apply adequate amount of pressure. She felt a little helpless and sad, but by now she had become used to all this. There were so many small things, which she was now being unable to do. She had learnt to start compromising with life for numerous small things, which had once upon a time mattered to her so much.

She decided to start practicing on her sketchbooks every day for a substantial amount of time. She also had to do the exercures, which the physiotherapist had taught her, for at least one hour every day. Her physiotherapist had also taught her some breathing exercise to help rebuilt her stamina which she had massively lost. She also decided that now that she is back home she would start doing the household chores like cooking, washing, cleaning, etc. to help her feel normal again.

However she was already tired and soon went off to sleep.

Rex was not yet home when she got up in the evening. She decided to practice a little on the sketchbook. She realized that despite of maximum effort, the weakness in her fingers did not allow her to draw properly.

Rex was not home even late in the night. As Carol lay on the bed and put on the television trying to keep herself awake until Rex was home, she soon fell asleep. It was the ringing of her mobile phone, which woke her up. As she woke up she tried to look around her to see the time. It was 1 am in the morning and she could not see Rex around. She tried to quickly pick up the phone when she saw her mother's name flashing on the phone screen. She was gripped by a sudden fear, a sort of impending doom because her mother never called her at this hour. With her heart beating fast, she spoke to her mother on the phone. The phone suddenly fell of her hand when she heard her mother speak. She could not believe what she had heard. With trembling hands she picked up the phone again to be absolutely certain regarding what her mother had told her. With a lump forming in her throat, Carol gathered courage to ask her mother, "Yes mom, tell me."

There was no answer from her mother's side, just sobs.

Carol asked again, "Mom, tell me what happened?"

Amidst loud sobs, Judy replied in a choking tone, "Carol, it was a massive heart attack, which David had. We did not even have the time to take him to the hospital."

Carol now realized that what her mother had told her in the beginning was the reality. Her father, David was dead. Carol froze on her bed for some time thinking about her father. Though she had stopped having any emotional attachment with him since long, she could not refute the fact that he had been responsible for bringing her in this world and that she did consider him as her dad since the time she was born. After some time when she came back to reality, she got up and looked around again to see if Rex was back. She could not see him anywhere. She called a cab and left for her mother's place.

In the morning when Carol came back home, Rex was already there. "Carol, your father passed away last night", Rex told Carol with hardly any trace of sadness in his voice.

"Hmmm, I know, I am coming from there only. Rex, I am surprised that you don't appear sad. You were pretty close to my father, weren't you?" asked Carol rather sternly.

"You were never on good terms with your father, so why should you really bother? Anyway, I have become the new owner of D&R architecture firm. In his will, David had transferred ownership of the company and his house to me," Rex said trying hard to hide the excitement in his voice.

"Rex, he was my father and my mother's husband and my mother loved him despite of his behaviour towards her," Carol said with sadness clearly visible in her voice. She was surprised that David had transferred the ownership of his house and office to Rex. "How Rex must have manipulated my father," wondered Carol. She also realized that all this while Rex must have been at the lawyer's place, while she had been busy performing the last rites for her father.

Soon she discovered that Rex was having a small party at home to celebrate his new ownership of the Company. He had called over a few people and ordered food and drinks from outside.

Carol wondered how heartless Rex could be. David was no longer with them and Rex was celebrating that he had become the new owner of David's firm. It was almost as if he was celebrating David's death. It appeared as if Rex had been desperately waiting for this to happen. Though it had been extremely painful for her, she had now come to terms with the fact that money was the only thing, which was important to Rex. It was only for money he had married Carol. Rex had taken control of David's architecture firm following his death. Now Carol understood that prior to their marriage Rex had been meeting David because he wanted to hypnotize him. Rex very well knew that Carol was not on good terms with her father. Also, she had no siblings so David was pretty likely to make Rex his inheritor if he appropriately manipulated him. He had very well succeeded in that and was now not only the new owner of her father's firm, but also her parent's house.

"*The lord answered all my questions and doubts:*
'I may make all things well; I can make all things well;
I will make all things well;
I shall make all things well; you shall see yourself
that all things shall be well"

—*Mother Julian of Norwich*
(1343-c.1416), England

CHAPTER 8

New Light

Carol was building a model with her hands. It was a model for a multi-storeyed departmental store. The window of the room where Carol was working was wide-open. Bright rays of sun were falling over the model, further glorifying its beauty. She was very happy with the design she had made. She had to show it to the clients to get it finalized. She tried lifting the model from the floor to the table. As she lifted the model, it suddenly slipped off her hands and fell on the floor. There was a loud sound as the model broke. The sound continued as Carol observed the model to be breaking into tiny pieces.

Suddenly Carol's eyes opened. The doorbell was ringing loudly. With her eyes half opened, she glanced at the clock. It was 4.30 am in the morning. It was still dark outside. She woke up Rex who was still sleeping on the bed to go and open the door.

"Who could come at this hour in the morning?" she wondered.

"Did you call the ambulance? Do you have an appointment with the neurologist today?" Rex asked her from the doorway.

"Yes I do, but the appointment was at 10 am," Carol replied, still not completely awake.

"I will check with them," replied Rex.

"They are saying, there has been some goof-up in the timings and they are here to pick you up for your appointment with Dr Humphreys," said Rex after clarifying with the ambulance driver.

"But it is still too early. Tell them to wait for some time. I will get ready," said Carol.

Three years had passed since Carol had suffered from transverse myelitis. Though the strength in her arms and legs had fully returned, she was still unable to do fine movements with the fingers of both the hands. After trying for few months, she eventually managed to procure a job at a small architecture firm. However, she was soon fired from her job because the owner of the firm did not feel that she would be able to give them perfect designs. Rex had many times persuaded Carol to join D&R architecture firm, but she had made it very clear that she did not want to work in the firm which had been first established by David.

Even though so many years had passed since Carol had been married to Rex, she was still not sure, if she understood Rex. He hardly spent any time with her.

Presently Carol had stopped asking Rex about his whereabouts even if he would not come home the entire night. All her physiotherapy and medicines had been stopped. Today was her last visit to the neurologist. Rex had stopped accompanying her during her hospital visits. Since she was not allowed to drive by herself, the hospital had taken the responsibility of arranging her visits by sending the ambulance.

Now she had known Dr Humphreys since the time had been undergoing treatment for transverse myelitis. He was a sweet man and had encouraged her in all her endeavours. She felt a little nostalgic that today would be her last visit to him.

Dr Humphreys had stopped all her medicines and exercises a few months back. "You still appear depressed", Dr Humphreys told Carol.

"This will continue for some time until I take control of my career. My career, which once had been the most important thing for me, is still unset," answered Carol.

"Carol, it is natural for patients with residual disability to experience several emotions. I can understand that at times you may be sad, frustrated, angry or even depressed. Such feelings are natural responses, but they can sometimes endanger your health and reduce the potential for functional recovery. I can prescribe you some antidepressants if you want. Do you want me to prescribe you some antidepressants?" Dr Humphreys kindly asked Carol.

"No, not at all," vehemently replied Carol. "I am strong enough to handle these things on my own. I don't want to get dependent on antidepressants."

"So what have you thought about your career?" Dr Humphreys asked again.

"To be very honest, I don't think I would be able to continue as an architect. I have an interest in singing. I was thinking about that because my voice is one thing, which has not at all been affected," Carol answered.

"Besides speech, your cognition and vision is also perfect", quipped Dr Humphreys.

"Yes, actually I have applied at the post of the lead singer in some local jigs. I am trying to seek some more professional help," Carol explained Dr Humphreys.

"Why don't you try talking to my wife? She has been a music teacher all her life. Now she has retired and takes music classes for both adults and children in the local church. She might be able to help you out. I will give you her mobile number," said Dr Humphreys thoughtfully.

"Definitely!" said Carol enthusiastically. "I would love to talk to her."

Carol left the clinic feeling happy and satisfied. Surprisingly she did not miss Rex today, nor did she think about him today. Even though she had come to terms with reality that some weakness in her hand may remain life long and she might never be able to practice as an architect, she was happy to know that she still has a way out, Mrs Dorothy Humphreys, Dr William

Humphrey's wife. While on the way back in the ambulance, Carol checked her purse with a child-like enthusiasm to check if the piece of paper on which Dr Humphreys had written his wife's number was still there. She smiled at herself as she tried to feel the paper with her fingers.

The health assistant accompanying Carol helped her open her home lock using the keys because she was still unable to do this herself. As soon as she reached her room, Carol called up Mrs Dorothy. Carol realised that Mrs Humphreys was a very soft-spoken and helpful woman. After hearing Carol's problem, she invited Carol to come to the local church where she normally took her classes. "Though I can say that you have a sweet voice on hearing you speak, I also want to hear you sing."

"I would love to meet you", quickly said Carol. "Tell me when do I come?"

"I usually hold my classes every Tuesday, 10 am in the morning in the music hall in the old church. You can come there any Tuesday," Dorothy informed Carol.

"Positively!" said Carol. "I got to go, because the doorbell is ringing. See you on next Tuesday. Bye and thanks so much for helping me out."

"It's been my pleasure speaking to you," replied Dorothy.

Carol quickly walked towards the door. She thought it might be Rex.

It indeed was Rex. "What took you so long to open the door?" barked Rex at Carol.

She got petrified, though the way Rex had started screaming at her for no reason, was not new to her. But she did feel bad because she had tried to open the door as soon as possible.

As soon as Carol opened the door, Rex just walked straight inside without looking at Carol. Suddenly, Carol heard the ringing of a mobile phone. Carol realised that it was Rex's phone which he had left on the table. While trying to pick it up, she saw Erica's name flashing on it. She wondered who Erica was? She had never heard this name ever in her life? Why was she calling up Rex?

Carol silently went inside the room and handed over the phone to Rex saying, "Rex, there is some Erica on the phone, I think she wants to speak to you."

"How do you know it is Erica? Did you speak to her?" asked Rex in an irritated tone his face red with anger.

"Rex, I wanted to ask you the same question, who is Erica?" questioned back Carol.

"She is nobody, just a business client. But why do you want to interfere in my life? Do I now start giving you an account of my business clients as well? When shall you ever stop bothering me, Carol?" Rex yelled out at Carol.

Carol had now become used to this rude, shouting and yelling by Rex. She silently left the room. However, she could not stop thinking. She could not help think if Rex had been actually telling her the truth. She was not sure if Rex had been telling her the truth regarding Erica just being his business client. Though Rex had been frequently losing his temper all this while, Carol had never seen him as angry as he was today. Suddenly she remembered DVD of the movie, 'P.S I love you', for which Rex had shown similar reaction. He had also abruptly blurted out the words 'Er'. "Did those words stand for Erica? If Erica did exist, why did Rex want to see a romantic movie with her?" Carol wondered, not really understanding the sequence of events. Suddenly Carol also realised that Rex had been on the phone quite too often since she had come home from the hospital. She had observed him awake in early hours of morning, 2 am, sometimes 3 am or 4 am talking to someone on the phone in the room adjacent to theirs. She had often asked him about whom he had been talking to. Every time he had scolded her saying, "it is none of your business."

Today she did not say anything. She silently laid down the lunch table. While having lunch she told Rex about Mrs Dorothy Humphreys.

Rex listened to Carol without showing any interest. He asked her rather rudely, "Why do you want to meet her?"

"She might be able to give me some advice about pursuing my career in music," patiently replied Carol.

"Why do want to pursue your career in music? Why do you always have to be self-centered and just think about yourself? I don't have any money to give you.

As it is, I have spent too much money on your illness. You have not been earning ever since you have fallen sick. Besides, you cannot earn your bread by singing. This would be useless for me," Rex blurted out with indifference.

Carol was deeply shocked. She had deeply loved Rex all these years despite his rude behaviour towards her. She knew she was not self-centered; she just wanted to build her career for her lost self-esteem.

"I want to be successful for both of us. Rex, you are worried about money and not about me. What happened to all your promises prior to marriage?" Carol tearfully questioned Rex.

Rex did not say anything. After a few minutes, he just left the room.

Though Carol had got a feeling about this all this while, today everything was crystal clear to her. She wanted to scream, but didn't. There was just a loud sob. Rex did not care. She could again hear him on the phone.

Now she had realised that Rex would probably never support her in building her career either in music or in architecture. She had realised that whatever she wanted, she would have to do it herself. She had now taken her decision. If her physical condition would not permit her to work as an architect, she would move into another stream. She had decided that now she would now follow her passion, music. She thought, "How easily Rex had stated that my career did not matter to him. How easily he had insulted my passion by saying that you cannot earn your bread from music."

His insult further strengthened Carol's decision. Her mind was now strongly determined to pursue her passion, music, which she now decided to make her life. She decided to meet Mrs Dorothy the coming Tuesday though Rex had not given his approval. She decided to plan out her further course of action only after consulting Mrs Dorothy.

Carol also realised that Rex had been behaving rather abruptly ever since she had been discharged home from the hospital. She recognized that his eyes had always been on David's property. Now that he had acquired what he wanted following David's death, he no longer needed her; in fact, she had become a burden for him.

"The love, which we had once shared no longer, exists," sadly thought Carol.

When and where love disappeared, she could not contemplate. However, she was sure that it was not there. Whether the love was still there from her side, she was not sure. She knew that until now she had deeply loved Rex, every moment, every day. She had unconditionally loved Rex from the beginning of her relationship. She was not sure of the circumstances, which had brought her away from Rex. But she could now join the threads. There had been mention of Erica at various instances. She wondered who Erica was. She was not even sure if Erica was the cause of their separation. Today she did not even care if Erica existed in reality or if it was only her imagination.

"I am not ready for a fake relationship where there is no love," she softly, but firmly spoke to herself. She had realised not everyone gets everything in life. Life had taken many things away from her. It was now for her to discover those things, which God had planned for her. She had taken a firm decision that she would begin her new life.

"Our plans fail because they have no aim.
For the sailor who does not know where to set
his course, there are no favourable winds"

—Seneca (4 BC-AD 65), Rome

CHAPTER 9

Soaring New Heights

It was a bright spring morning. The winters had not fully gone and therefore the morning air was still chilly. White and yellow daffodils lining the pavement on both the sides seemed to dance with joy as the morning wind brushed past them.

Carol walked past the pavements, humming at herself. Today she felt happy. All the doubts had cleared off from her mind. She felt free as a bird. As the wind moved past her through her hair and face, she moved her hand through her hair to prevent it from coming over her eyes. She realized that her fingers were not able to pass completely through her hair. For a moment she thought about her illness. Soon, however, her mind drifted away in her own thoughts. It was going to be a new beginning for her from her, starting today. She took some time to reach the old church because it had been a long time since she had walked out of the house alone. Since her legs would still get unsteady at times, the physiotherapist had advised her against walking alone for long distances. But today she did not care, about Rex or about the physiotherapist or even about her not being able to practice as an architect. Today, she felt she was getting liberated. She would be getting a chance to pursue her passion, music.

The church building though beautiful appeared uninhabited. Her thoughts were suddenly interrupted by the sound of piano notes coming from inside. She entered inside and saw an elderly lady playing piano. She was singing lines of a hymn. A group of 10-15 people, both men and women were standing in a group and singing in rounds. Carol stood there listening to the song awestruck. Since she also knew the lyrics, she started softly humming the song herself. The song finished, but Carol wanted to hear more. It was indeed pure harmony. She realized that the woman playing the piano must be Mrs Dorothy. Carol had taken an immediate liking for her because she reminded her of her late grandmother with whom she had been extremely attached. She went to Mrs Dorothy and presented herself. Mrs Dorothy was extremely warm and pleasant in welcoming Carol and introduced her to the group of her students. Though most of them appeared to be over 50 years of age and Carol appeared to be the youngest one in the group, all of them were extremely helpful and encouraging. Carol did not even for once felt out of place. She was offered some coffee and cookies by one of the ladies in the group. Dorothy then called her, and gently said, "Carol I realise you have been facing a very tough time since past few years. Sit down and tell me all about your problem."

Carol after sitting down on a chair next to Dorothy honestly replied, "Well Dorothy, I am basically an architect. I do not think I shall be able to do complete justification to my job as an architect after my illness. Music had always been my passion right from the childhood. I think now I want to make music my life because I think it is a kind of job, which I would be able to completely justify. My sickness has not at all affected my speech, hearing, vision and cognition.

Dorothy ran her fingers through Carol's hair and affectionately said, "Carol I want to hear you sing."

Carol quickly asked, "Should I sing the same song which your group was singing when I entered the room?"

"Sure, why not. The group will join you in the chorus," Dorothy replied.

Dorothy started playing the notes of the song on the piano. Carol kept sitting on the chair and sang one stanza. For the chorus the group joined. The whole scene was mesmerizing. Mrs Dorothy kept on playing the piano; Carol kept on singing one stanza after the other and the group kept accompanying her for the chorus. Mrs Dorothy was playing notes of the piano as if a beautiful colourful butterfly was gracefully moving from one beautiful flower to another. Carol's singing appeared as if another fragile beauty was spreading her wings towards the beautiful skies to take whatever the life brings with it. The chorus appeared as if a group of birds were trying to soar higher and higher, exploring life and becoming something more than one might have ever imagined. It appeared as if Carol was declaring to the world that she would not be conforming to the worldly pattern, but following her heart and transforming her world through it.

After the song finished everyone clapped.

Dorothy said, "Carol that was beautiful". Other people present in the room congratulated and praised Carol.

Dorothy hugged Carol and said, "Carol you were excellent and you definitely have the potential. But I want you to get even more refined in your singing. I would like to give you some lessons. Is that all right?"

"Definitely, Dorothy, I completely trust you in whatever you say. But if you don't mind can I ask you one thing?" Carol asked.

"Sure darling," said Dorothy

"What would be your fees?" asked Carol with doubt in her voice.

Everyone present in the room including Dorothy started laughing.

"I do this for charity, sweetheart. I just charge one dollar per hour so that I can arrange some coffee and cookies for all of you and pay rent for this place. Will that be okay with you?" Dorothy replied calmly.

"Oh sure, I will definitely come every Tuesday for practice," Carol assured Dorothy.

From that day onwards, Carol started focussing completely on her music practice. She would get up early in the morning and start practicing her music. Rex would get irritated with her and rebuked her several times for concentrating on her music practice. She, however, remained determined and focused and continued with her practice sessions regularly every day. She also continued to attend her training sessions with Mrs Dorothy Humphreys every Tuesday without any failure. Mrs Dorothy was really impressed by Carol's determination and willpower.

During one of the Tuesday classes, Dorothy told Carol, "Carol, there is some good news for you!"

Excited Carol asked, "Dorothy what is it? Please tell me soon."

"We are having the annual charity fair after 2 months. Our group has been chosen to give a performance there. I want you to be the lead singer," Dorothy said.

The group of singers cheered out loudly.

"Oh! That is great Dorothy!" replied Carol in an excited tone. Carol felt excited at the thought of being the lead singer in front of a big audience. However, soon she started thinking about the relevance of appearing in a charity event.

"But I really don't understand how this shall help me?" Carol asked Dorothy with confusion clearly showing in her voice.

"Look Carol, it is for charity so you would have to perform for free. Though there would be no monetary benefit, you would be performing in front of a big audience so there is a high probability for recognition. There is a very good chance that someone out there in the audience may recognize your talent and give you your first entry ticket into the world of music," explained Dorothy serenely.

Carol was excited and thought that she would share this news to Rex even though she knew that he may not really be interested or happy about this. Despite of this, as soon as Carol reached her home, she could not stop herself from calling up Rex on his mobile. As she had already expected, Rex did not at all appear concerned about her endeavours. However, this did not dishearten Carol. She called up Judy on her mobile.

On the phone Judy told Carol, "Darling, I would be more than happy to help you. As it is, I have always encouraged your singing activities."

Though Carol already knew about this, she was pleased to hear her mother's words.

"Mom, I already knew about this. Now that I have both you and Dorothy by my side, I am sure that I shall be successful," Carol said happily.

"God bless you Carol," replied Judy as she cut the phone line.

After having spoken to her mother, Carol tried charting out a plan for starting her music practice. For the following few weeks Carol focused her mind completely on her singing. She took regular training from both Dorothy and Judy. During this time, Carol completely stopped thinking about Rex. She concentrated entirely on her singing. There were times when Rex would not even come back home the whole night. Carol now even refrained herself from asking his whereabouts during the nights. After practicing her singing day and night, the day of the event eventually arrived.

Carol reached the hall where her performance was to take place. As she had expected, Rex had refused to accompany her, so she reached there alone. When she arrived, the hall was jam-packed. Though Dorothy had said that this was a charity event, the crowd out there was unbelievable. Besides Carol's performance, there had been several other music and dance performances throughout the day. There also had been exhibitions on hand-drawn paintings, hand-made dolls and soft toys and handmade chocolates. All the money collected through sale of these items was to be donated to a charity, which took care of homeless children. Carol felt happy to see so many people because more tickets being bought implied that the amount of money collected to be donated to the charity would be high. At the same time her heart sank because she had never sang in front of so many people ever in her life before. All her fears disappeared when she looked at Dorothy and Judy. Both of them had that bright gleam in their eyes, which reflected their trust and confidence in Carol. This made

Carol forget all her fears. This was one of those times when Dorothy reminded Carol of her late grandmother. She regained her lost spirit and confidently moved towards the dais for her performance.

As Carol walked towards the mike, the palms of her hands felt cold and clammy; her head felt lightheaded and her legs felt tight. Her mind went racing and a vague fear gripped her that something bad was going to happen. Then as she heard the audience cheering and calling out her name, she tried to regain control of herself. She reminded herself of her passion and goal in life. She also calmed herself by thinking, "I have practiced enough to forget the lyrics of my song so why should I worry?" Carol had recovered her lost confidence by the time she reached the mike. As she held the mike, she was in total control of the situation. Lyrics of the first stanza flowed in easily, just the way it had done when Carol had given her audition to Dorothy. Carol's voice musically sounded great as it echoed through the hall. Besides Carol's voice, there was pin drop silence in the hall and the audience sat motionless, listening to her mesmerized.

By the time, Carol reached the next stanza, she felt as if she was again losing out on her confidence. She gave a look towards the audience and smiled at them. Through the corner of her eyes she noticed Dorothy and Judy smiling back at her. This gave Carol the strength to really reach out and grab the audience. She sang with all her strength and determination, one stanza after the other. Soon Carol realized that she was on the last line. She had finally finished her performance, the performance in which she had put her everything, her mind, her soul, her spirit and her heart. After finishing her performance Carol stood on the stage for a few seconds to see the reaction of the audience.

There was no reaction.

No sound, not even a clap by a single soul.

"The greatest deception men suffer is from their own opinions."

—*Leonardo DaVinci*

CHAPTER 10

Deception

It was 5 am in the morning. Rex woke up. Though his eyes were yet not completely open, half asleep he looked around himself. His head was badly hurting. There was no one on the bed besides him. The sheets on the adjacent bed had been clumsily wrapped up. There were numerous wrinkles on the bed sheet, suggesting that someone had been lying there a while ago. Rex then tried to envisage the series of events, which may have occurred.

"Where is Erica?" suddenly thought Rex. He remembered that he had brought Erica to the private cabin in his office, last night. It was not only last night that he had been here with Erica but also he had been with her for several nights and several days previously. She was rich, stylish, attractive and single, at least Rex thought so. He realised that it had been getting increasingly difficult for him to handle both Carol and Erica. However, he had chosen to spend more time with Erica.

Rex had met Erica in a pub one day where he had gone to de-stress, when Carol was in the hospital. While Rex was sitting on the table waiting for the waiter to come with the order, he observed a young couple sitting on the corner table. They appeared to be in a relationship.

Rex looked at the girl, she was stunningly beautiful. He started thinking about Carol. Soon he was lost in thoughts thinking about Carol and how much she had been suffering due to her illness. He thought about the good times they had spent together. Suddenly his mind went blank. The series of events which had occurred over the past few days passed across his eyes all over again. Rex sat in the pub, thinking about Carol's phone call, her mention about her illness; then she being taken to the hospital and eventually being diagnosed with transverse myelitis. Rex's thoughts were suddenly interrupted by loud voices coming from the nearby table. Initially the conversation between the couple on the nearby table was in form of whispers, which had now been replaced by loud arguments. Amidst these loud arguments, the man who had been previously accompanying the beautiful girl had left the table. The girl was left alone on the table sobbing. Rex could hear her loud sobs. Soon there were voices of argument between the girl and the waiter. Her husband had abruptly left her and apparently she had no money with her. Soon the hotel's manager also arrived at the scene. The poor girl did not know what to and how to pay for the food and drinks they had ordered. Rex who had been all the time watching the scene, somehow felt obliged to help the girl out. He walked up to the hotel manager and asked him how much the bill was.

"Fifty dollars, sir," the manager replied.

"They are troubling this girl for only 50 dollars?!" Rex thought as he reached out to the pocket of his trousers and from his wallet, took out a 50 dollar bill, which he handed over to the waiter. The waiter and the manager immediately left the scene. The girl who had been taken with surprise looked at Rex with an expression of gratitude in her eyes. As Rex caught her eye, he suddenly felt a little self-conscious and said quickly, "this was nothing Miss . . . .

"Erica, Erica Custer," the girl spontaneously replied, immediately completing what Rex had to say.

"Okay Erica, don't worry about what happened. Do you want me to give you a lift till somewhere?" Rex politely asked her.

"It would be great if you could just drop me to the station. I have a train pass. I would be able to reach home using that," Erica quickly replied.

"Are you sure?" Rex asked with concern.

"Yes absolutely," Erica answered.

"Okay, keep my mobile number with you. Give me a call if you ever need my help," Rex said handing over his card to Erica as he left.

Rex had to reach the hospital where Carol was admitted. As soon as Rex's car was out of sight, the man who had been accompanying Erica in the hotel, appeared from behind the trees. He held Erica's hand. They both treacherously smiled at one another as they left together hand-in-hand.

Many days passed following this incident. Rex had nearly forgotten about Erica, when one day he received a call from Erica. She wanted to meet Rex. Rex agreed on meeting Erica. After fixing up the meeting with Erica, he himself was surprised regarding why he had agreed to meet her. There was something enticing about her and her voice, which allured Rex towards her. Several other meetings followed that meeting and soon Rex was spending a substantial amount of time with her. He had started neglecting Carol and had started giving increasing amount of preference to Erica. Using her charms Erica had succeeded in attracting Rex towards herself. She had succeeded in manipulating Rex for transferring nearly half of his salary into her account every month. Rex, totally ignorant of her ulterior motives, had been transferring funds into her account every month since past two years. In fact, he had been so mesmerized by Erica that he had mentally prepared himself to leave Carol and marry her. Carol had become more of a liability rather than help. In fact, Rex had already obtained what he wanted from Carol. Presently, she was of no use for him.

Now Rex was completely awake. Rex tried hard to remember the series of events which may have occurred when he was last with Erica. Today he had proposed Erica, asking her to marry him. She had looked at him with a strange expression, which he could not understand at that time. Now as Rex lay alone in the bed, he got feeling that probably Erica had no intention of marrying him. She was probably just after his money.

However, he did not want to believe that. Instead he consoled himself explaining that probably she has left for some really urgent work early in the morning. "Where can Erica go at 5 am in the morning?" Rex mused. He tried calling up her mobile, but it was switched off. Rex looked around the table searching for his car keys. He could not find them. He fumbled through his pocket, looking for his wallet. However, he could not even find that. He realized that all his credit cards were gone. The keys of his locker, which contained the ownership papers of his house and business, were also gone. Giving Erica a benefit of doubt, he frantically looked in the drawers and cupboards with the hope that he might find the files containing the ownership papers of the business and house there. However, they were not even there.

Completely perplexed and clueless, Rex sat down on the sofa trying to figure out what had happened. He remembered being with Erica last night. They both had decided to spend the night together. Erica had insisted that they stay in Rex's private cabin in his office rather than her house because she was afraid that her husband could come there any time. When together, she had served him some wine. He could not recollect how many glasses she made him have, but he did remember that he suddenly felt drowsy after drinking that. His head was still hurting. A new realization suddenly hit Rex. Probably, something had been mixed in the wine. Rex rose from his chair towards the dining table. The empty wine glass was still lying on the table. When Rex checked it, he realized that there was some white powdery deposit at the bottom. Soon Rex realized that Erica must have mixed some sedative in his wine and had taken his business and property papers with her.

He still did not want to believe that Erica had fooled him. So he started looking around the room to look for some clue. He found a neatly folded paper note beneath his pillow. He frantically opened the piece of paper to see what had been written on it. The first thing he noted was that it had been signed by Erica. She had written, "Rex I hated David, he had deceived my mother whom he had promised to marry. He had been cheating upon Judy all his life and you very well knew about all this, Rex. When he refused to marry my mom, he had sworn to transfer his business and property to my husband. Here again he deceived us, so we had devised a plan to take our revenge on him. Since you had become the owner of David's business and house, you were bound to become our scapegoat. Sorry about that, but no sorry because you anyways deserved it."

Signed
Erica

Soon after reading the message written on the paper, Rex, fuming with anger, tore the paper into small pieces and flung it in air.

"If you don't get everything you want, think of the things you don't get that you don't want"

—*Oscar Wilde (1854-1900), Ireland*

CHAPTER 11

The Heart Shall Never Bleed Again

Carol had not seen Rex since the past week. She had sent him a text message on the day of her charity performance, requesting him to come and see her music performance. However, he had not come. Even though so many days had passed since her performance, she in her thoughts could not forget that day of her performance. Her music concert had really been successful. She could not help not to recall the sequence of events that had occurred that day. Carol could not help remember the initial stage fright, then the way she overcame it and gave an extremely powerful performance. She remembered the immediate pin drop silence from the audience following her performance. However, soon afterwards, there was a loud applause from the audience which continued for nearly 5-10 minutes, with the audience asking for more. Carol's mother and Dorothy appeared extremely happy with her performance. However, all three of them knew that this was not enough. Carol still required someone to recognize her talent and give her a contract for some key singing assignment. None of them knew when it would come and whether it would ever come also or not? All they could do at that time was just to wait and watch . . . .

Few months had passed since Carol's charity performance. Though she had not acquired any major music contract, she had got a few isolated small singing assignments. Carol had now made her decision. She had found a direction in life. She did not need anybody's help to pursue it. She decided to follow her passion by herself. With a heavy heart, she thought, "I don't even need to stay with Rex to carry on."

She sadly thought of the time when Rex had told her, "From now on, you shall never be alone. You will always have someone to help pursue your dreams. When ever you need me just close your eyes and think about me. I shall be there." But now, he was never there whenever she wanted him. Lately Carol had noticed that Rex would not come home even during the nights. Carol had now even stopped thinking about where Rex could be. Thinking about Rex, Carol opened the window of her room. There was total darkness outside and not a single star could be seen in the sky.

Days rolled by . . . .

One day Carol was sleeping in the afternoon, when she was suddenly woken up from her sleep by the ringing of her phone.

Still not fully alert, she drowsily picked up the phone.

"Is that Mrs Carol Harrison?" the voice over the phone asked.

"Yes, this is Carol speaking," replied Carol. She had now stopped mentioning any surname, Wilde or Harrison with her name. Now she was just Carol.

"We have some good news for you," replied the voice on phone. "I am Betsy Matthews, the HR manager in a non-profit organization, which works for the welfare of adults with neurological diseases. We have an offer for you," continued the voice.

"Yes, please tell me," Carol asked

"We would like you to sign a contract for being the lead singer at a major charity event, which is organized by our society," replied Betsy.

"What???" Uttered Carol.

"Yes, that's right, you are being appointed as the lead singer for the charity events organized by the neurological society," confirmed Betsy. "You are requested to come to our office to sign the contract within this week," added Betsy.

"Thanks, I shall definitely come. Tell me the address," replied Carol.

After keeping down the phone, as an instinct, Carol inadvertently closed her eyes as if she was thanking her lucky stars. She definitely wanted to be associated with a society working towards the welfare of young adults with neurological diseases, something of which she herself had been a victim and which had changed her life as well. Then she opened her eyes again and looked around herself. Rex was not there in the house. She could not even remember when she had last seen him. However, the truth was out. Carol had discovered herself as a singer. She realized that this was just the beginning and she had a long way to go. Today her singing has just been appreciated and she has only got an offer as the lead singer for a non-profit organization. This was not her goal, but a step forward towards achieving her aim of becoming a singer of international acclaim. She immediately called up Dorothy and Judy to tell them both about the good news.

She was not sure if she should call up Rex to share the news with him. Thinking about his probable reaction, she decided otherwise. She realized that today was her day of liberation. She would let all her fears go away. Her biggest fear, she realized, was the fear of losing Rex. Today she vowed to herself that would let him go too. She had earlier thought that Rex and her lives were both linked together. However, this was not destined to happen. She gracefully accepted the destiny and decided not to interfere with it. She realized that Rex and she were now living as two separate individuals, each having a life and desires of their own. Both of them should be left on their own. She decided that she would no longer stay with Rex. She called up Dorothy on phone and told her, "Dorothy today I have found my true joy behind living. I just need to seek your blessings towards further developing my singing skills."

"Carol you very well know I have not just appreciated, but absolutely loved your singing. I shall always be there to help you out with your singing as long as I am alive. God bless you in your goals," Dorothy affectionately told Carol.

Carol packed her basic belongings. As Carol looked around the house to see that she had not missed out on anything essential, she saw her old sketchbooks lying on the table. With a heavy heart she thought of those days when she was practicing as an architect and would spend hours together working on the designs. She wiped a tear in her eye and took control of the situation by explaining herself, "I shall not worry about the things life has taken away from me. I shall bring joy in my life from the things I already have or those whom I would soon acquire."

As Carol moved around the house to make sure that she had not left some essential item, her eye caught attention of a photo frame, staring at her. It had Rex's and her name written on it in form of cross-stitch pattern, which she herself had made just before their marriage. She immediately gripped the photo frame. Since she could not obtain a strong grip over the frame, it slipped off her hands and fell on the ground. She carefully grasped the cloth with cross-stitch design on it, lying amongst the shreds of the glass frame on the floor. Grasping the cloth in her hand, she went into the kitchen. With a great amount of effort, she picked up a match box and struck a match stick. Without thinking twice, Carol immediately ignited the cloth having the cross-stitch design with a lit match stick. Within a matter of few seconds the cloth caught flames. The entire cloth burnt up turning into thin black flakes of ash. Carol let the flakes of ash fall on the floor. Leaving the ash which had fallen on the ground, she walked towards the door with a strong determination.

As Carol put her foot outside the house, she paused for a second and looked around herself. Everything appeared same as before. The trees were the same. The birds chirping on the trees were the same. However, today there was something special in everything she saw around herself. Once she left her household, she did not even once turned back to see what she had left. She walked out of the house without a tear in her eye or any regret in her mind. Life is beautiful; she thought and looked above towards the sky. There were a million of stars in the sky today and all of them were twinkling with all their might and appeared to be smiling at her. She had understood that life is the gift of God and tomorrow may or may not hold new promises, but she was happy. She walked forwards with a sparkle in her eyes, never to look back again.

Picture Courtesy: Debjeet Kundu

Epilogue

Many years later . . . . .

Carol opened the window of her room to let the broad rays of sun come in. The sunshine loomed in to form a bright patch over the duvet lying over a large bed. Huddled underneath the duvet was 5-year-old little Dorothy.

"Dorothy, wake up! It is time to go to school. You shall miss your bus again." Carol tried to wake up Dorothy. Carol was now working full time as the lead singer in a big music company. She had rented a large apartment where she had been living with Judy. Though many a times she had an urge to call up Rex, she had always stopped herself from calling and asking him about how his life had been going on. Few years after Judy's death, she had adopted a little 6-month-old girl child whom she had named as Dorothy as a symbol of respect and affection she had for the old woman, whom Carol believed to have changed her life.

After initial few minutes of throwing tantrums, Dorothy woke up and got ready for school. While Carol was accompanying Dorothy on her way to the bus stop, they both passed through the pond. Little Dorothy while walking stopped at the poolside bending down to see the flowing waters. Carol too stopped at the pond side and told Dorothy, "Baby, see those pigeons sitting on the rope over the water. The last time I was here, most of them were perched on the rope and they were trying to fly. Today you can see that most of them have been successfully able to fly."

"Mom, what does that mean?" Dorothy asked Carol.

"This means that no matter what problems come in life, you must keep going ahead with all your determination," replied Carol.

"Determination? means?" questioned little Dorothy in child-like language, with a confused look on her face.

"Determination means keep trying until you succeed." Carol replied, suddenly realizing that Dorothy may be too small to understand. "Never mind Dorothy, one day you shall understand," said Carol in an audible voice.

"Mom, I am a good girl, I have already understood," Dorothy replied trying to sound clever.

"That's my girl and that's the way I want you to be," said Carol embracing Dorothy in her arms and lightly kissing her on her forehead.